Hannah Elizabeth

pictures by Paul Edward Kennedy

Hannah Elizabeth

by Elaine Sommers Rich

HARPER & ROW, PUBLISHERS
New York, Evanston, and London

The second stanza of "Extol the Love of Christ" by S. F. Coffman, from the Mennonite CHURCH HYMNAL, reprinted on page 123 with the permission of the Mennonite Publishing House.

HANNAH ELIZABETH. Copyright © 1964 by Elaine Sommers Rich. Printed in the United States of America. All rights reserved. No part of this book may be used or reproduced in any manner whatsoever without written permission except in the case of brief quotations embodied in critical articles and reviews. For information address Harper & Row, Publishers, Incorporated, 49 East 33rd Street, New York 16, N. Y.
Library of Congress catalog card number: 64-12024

Dedicated
to my parents and grandparents

❧ Contents

And he shewed me a pure river of water of life, clear as crystal, proceeding out of the throne of God and of the Lamb . . . And the Spirit and the bride say, Come. And let him that heareth say, Come. And let him that is athirst come. And whosoever will, let him take the water of life freely.

—REVELATION 22:1 and 17

Hannah Elizabeth

ONE

Shrock Reunion Day

What did the words mean? Ten-year-old Hannah Elizabeth Shrock sat on the wooden church bench of the Mennonite meetinghouse listening to Grandfather Shrock read the opening Scripture lesson.

God is our refuge and strength,
   a very present help in trouble.
Therefore will not we fear,
   though the earth be removed,
   and though the mountains be carried
     into the midst of the sea;

1

Though the waters thereof roar and be troubled,
though the mountains shake
with the swelling thereof. Selah.
There is a river,
the streams whereof shall make glad
the city of God,
the holy place of the tabernacles
of the most High. . . .

Although the cadence of the words entranced Hannah Elizabeth, she puckered her forehead, as she often did, for she had many things to wonder about and figure out.

There is a river, the streams whereof shall make glad the city of God.

What river was it? Surely not an Indiana river like the Mississinewa, the Wabash or the Wildcat. Perhaps it was not a river at all. And perhaps the city was not Kokomo or Peru. The Bible was like that. It was hard to understand. She sighed gently. So much to find out.

Hannah Elizabeth Shrock wanted to be a poet when she grew up. But she had never breathed a word of this secret ambition, not even to Cousin Rachel. Why? Well, after all, she was only a scrawny, skinny, ugly, awkward little girl. She had purplish freckles on her nose. Maybe not purplish, but quite disfiguring. Could a poet have disfiguring freckles? Whatever she touched with her hands, except piano keys, either tangled or broke. Life sometimes seemed troublesome indeed to her. How could she tell people she wanted to be a poet? They would laugh. Poets were tall, graceful, willowy and beautiful. Oh, dear, her mind was wandering again. She should be paying more attention to the church service.

Hannah Elizabeth brightened when Uncle Paton, the chorister, announced that the congregation would now sing hymn number twenty-five. Good! Hannah Elizabeth's favorite, "Joyful, Joyful, We Adore Thee." And it was Grandfather's favorite too. She sang with gusto. The words and music seemed to lift her toward heaven, a heaven surprisingly like an Indiana woods in springtime, with birds singing and wild flowers blooming. The bass, tenor, alto and

soprano voices blended into one and floated through the open windows over the surrounding cornfields. No organ or piano accompanied the singing.

These were plain people. The women had long hair and wore no hats or rings. They drove cars and had electricity in their homes. Except for a few older ones, the men were smooth-shaven. Many of the people, including Hannah Elizabeth's parents, could speak or understand Pennsylvania Dutch, the dialect their forebears had brought from Europe to Pennsylvania before the American Revolution. They tried hard to maintain a difference between their church and the "world." In Europe, Mennonite migrations had been caused by religious persecution. In the United States their movement had followed the flow to the west.

The August Sunday-morning church service ended. A friendly buzz of conversation began, and Hannah Elizabeth Shrock, would-be poet, was only a small girl in a sea of uncles, aunts, cousins and friends. The grownups were greeting one another, exchanging community news and conferring about plans for the coming week. Hannah Elizabeth had some urgent business of her own to transact. At last she spied her beautiful cousin Rachel in the after-meeting crowd.

Lo and behold, the two cousins had been thinking about exactly the same thing, for they said to each other almost simultaneously, "Just five more days until Shrock Reunion!"

"When can we practice?" Hannah Elizabeth wanted to know.

"I've been wondering what we will do if

Cousin Eva doesn't ask us this year. Will your mother get our dresses done? Do the skirts really have sixteen gores?" Rachel too had questions.

Hannah Elizabeth frowned. Such dire possibilities! What indeed would they do if Cousin Eva did not ask? Rachel was not only beautiful, she was positively practical.

"I'm sure Mother will get the dresses done," Hannah Elizabeth assured her cousin. "What I'm worried about is whether the Great Debut will be a success."

The Great Debut, planned by the two girls at Hannah Elizabeth's tenth birthday celebration just two weeks before, was to be the occasion when two new stars burst into the firmament.

"Let's get prepared and then live in hope," Rachel suggested sensibly.

The wheels in Hannah Elizabeth's head kept turning. "We'd better ask your mother whether you can come home with me. If I go with you, we'll have to bother with Paul."

Paul! Ugh! Both girls grimaced. Rachel's older brother, Paul, would spoil everything.

Hannah Elizabeth's three younger ones would not realize what was going on.

So it was that Cousin Rachel Shrock went home with Hannah Elizabeth's family to the crossroads town of Liberty for the afternoon. After dinner and dishwashing the two girls sang and played the same song over and over at the piano.

Once Hannah Elizabeth's little brother Tim caught them bending and bowing. "What are you girls doing?" he asked, mystified, for he did not understand that they were curtsying to a large imaginary audience.

"Nothing," Hannah Elizabeth said evasively, and they waited until he had left the room before continuing the practice.

Rachel rejoined her own family at the evening church service, and the two cousins began a week of agitated waiting.

The following Saturday morning, Shrock Reunion Day, dawned clear and sunshiny. Hannah Elizabeth put on the new dress with its sixteen-gored skirt and gave it a twirl. Of course Mother

Shrock had completed the dresses in time and had sent Rachel's along home with Uncle 'Lijah and Aunt Ellen, Rachel's parents, when they stopped in Liberty Thursday afternoon on their way home from town. Hannah Elizabeth practiced holding her head high. If only she were beautiful like Rachel! Rachel was a head taller than she, had brown wavy hair and not one freckle on her creamy skin.

The Bible said that true beauty was inside a person. *The ornament of a meek and quiet spirit.* But that kind of beauty did not show on a stage. What was she to do? She would simply be as graceful and dignified as possible under the circumstances.

Hannah Elizabeth brushed her teeth vigorously with salt and soda until they shone. She did not consider her family poor, but she did wish they could afford to buy a tube of toothpaste for use on such special days. Toothpaste and a new dictionary—those were the two things, other than beauty, that she really needed.

What would happen to the Great Debut if

Cousin Eva did not ask this year? The thought was so disturbing that Hannah Elizabeth brushed it from her mind as vigorously as she had brushed her teeth.

At eleven o'clock Hannah Elizabeth's and Rachel's families joined hundreds of cousins— first, second, third and once-removed—in trekking to the reunion park. Once a year members of this Mennonite-Dunkard-Quaker clan forgot their differences on baptism—pouring, immersion or no water at all. Family ties were uppermost.

Eager to find Rachel, Hannah Elizabeth tumbled out of the car. She did not appreciate the almost unknown relatives, cousins of Grandfather Shrock, who said politely to her, "You must be Susan and Mark's girl! How old are you?"

Her eyes were searching for the sixteen-gored skirt that matched hers. "Ten," she replied, trying to be polite also.

"What grade will you be in?"

"Fifth."

"What do you want to be when you grow up?"

Her brow puckered. "I don't know."

Why did grownups always ask these same three boring questions, Hannah Elizabeth wondered, looking frantically for Rachel. "How old are you? What grade will you be in? What do you want to be when you grow up?" It would not be nice to ask them how old they were, even if you cared. It was terrible to lie like that and say she did not know what she wanted to be. She knew perfectly well. But to tell the truth! She could not do it.

Suddenly a great upsurge of character and a sense of adventure overcame Miss Hannah Elizabeth Shrock. "I will do it," she said to herself. "To the next person who asks me what I want to be when I grow up, I will tell the truth, the whole truth and nothing but the truth."

The desperate resolution made, she shivered with delight and ran to join Rachel, whom she had just seen at the sliding board. Meanwhile the mothers placed the bounteous reunion dinner on four wooden tables placed end to end.

When she had at last joined her cousin, Hannah Elizabeth said to Rachel in heartfelt admiration, "You look just ravishingly beautiful." It was humiliating to be so ugly and freckled. Just humiliating! It was a wonder Rachel consented to appear on the same platform with her.

"Well, you don't look exactly beautiful, but you sure do know a lot of words," Rachel replied loyally. "And you'd better know how to play the piano."

Hannah Elizabeth was suddenly cold with fear now that she could share what she was thinking with her cousin. She half whispered, "Rachel, what if Cousin—"

"I saw her talking to Great-Aunt Elmira Shrock just now," Rachel said confidently. "Why don't we just *tell* her about the Great Debut?"

"We wouldn't dare ask her," Hannah Elizabeth said hastily. "It would be too bold and brazen."

The girls' problem was solved when Cousin

Eva herself appeared with notebook and pencil in hand and got right to the point. "Do you girls have something for the program this afternoon?"

Hannah Elizabeth's spirit soared with relief.

"Yes, we do," Rachel said straightforwardly. "I'm going to sing a solo, and . . ."

"I'm going to ac-com-pan-y her on the piano," the second cousin added, pronouncing each syllable carefully.

"That's fine!" Cousin Eva beamed, and she jotted a memo into her little black notebook. Cousin Eva had been secretary and program chairman of the Shrock Reunion for more years than either Hannah Elizabeth or Rachel could remember. She had asked them this same question every year. "Do you girls have something for the program?" Until this year, when they were ten, they had never been grown-up enough to realize that the question could have more than one answer.

"How you girls have grown!" Cousin Eva said, treating the Great Debut with incredible matter-of-factness. "What do you want to be when you grow up?"

"A nurse," Rachel replied.

"And you?"

Hannah Elizabeth breathed deeply. This was it. She summoned every bit of courage she could muster.

"A poet."

"How nice," Cousin Eva said casually. "I like pieces myself."

Hannah Elizabeth blinked at her. Was that all there was to it?

When the many relatives had eaten—fried chicken, ham, bologna sandwiches, noodles, mashed potatoes, green beans, baked beans, potato salad, bean salad, coleslaw, raw tomato and cucumber slices, pickles (dill, sweet, bread-and-butter), celery, fruit (peaches, watermelon, cantaloupe, grapes), puddings (tapioca, pineapple, date, chocolate), pie (ground-cherry, apple, raisin, peach, banana, pumpkin), cake (angel, chocolate, yellow, marble)—the group gathered on the wooden benches in the program shell of the park. Great-Uncle M.S. (for Menno Simons) Shrock was master of ceremonies as usual. He cleared his throat, and the visiting quieted down. Hannah Elizabeth and Rachel sat beside Grandfather and Grandmother Shrock.

"It's time to begin our program, folks," Great-Uncle M.S. said. "I've asked Cousin Joseph to open with prayer." Everyone stood, and Grandfather thanked God briefly for "dear ones who have completed their lives on earth and gone home to Thee" and for "the sweet fellowship we have with one another." Hannah Elizabeth was now a tremolo of excitement. The Great Debut was at hand.

Great-Uncle M.S. read a list of people who had died during the year, and people who had married and babies that had been born. He asked the oldest person in the audience to stand and tell what he remembered of the reunion fifty years ago. He asked who was the youngest person in the audience. "A silly thing to do," thought Hannah Elizabeth. "Of course it will be a baby, and how can a—?" But before she could finish her thought, a proud grandmother with a sleeping baby on her large lap said, "My grandson Jacob Joseph Junior is six weeks old today!" Sure enough! Jacob Joseph Junior Shrock was the youngest person in the audience.

"We need to be acquainted with our heritage," Great-Uncle M.S. continued in his preacherlike voice. "We need to appreciate our forefathers. They came to this country for religious freedom. They did not want to belong to a state church. They wished to follow the dictates of their own consciences. They were pioneers. Often I have heard Grandfather tell of how he and Grandmother came with a yoke of oxen and their household goods all the way from Tuscarawas County, Ohio. They followed the Wabash River to Peru and then come overland to the southern part of Miami County."

A woman near Hannah Elizabeth yawned. Great-Uncle M.S. was long-winded when he talked about family history. After what seemed to Rachel and Hannah Elizabeth an intolerably

15 ✒

long time, he at last turned the meeting over to Cousin Eva. She mentioned how pleased everyone always was to hear from the "younger generation" and said the audience had a "real treat in store this afternoon." They would now hear a solo by Rachel Shrock, accompanied at the piano by Hannah Elizabeth Shrock.

Oh, to be beautiful for just fifteen minutes! The Great Debut had come. Scrawny, ugly little Hannah Elizabeth wiped her moist hands on her sixteen-gored skirt and followed tall, beautiful, graceful Rachel. Neither of them noticed a long rusty nail protruding from one end of the third wooden step to the platform.

Hours of practice had had their effect. Hannah Elizabeth struck the first notes as though she were at home alone in the living room or in a concert hall. The piano was out of tune. It bothered her, but the audience did not seem to mind. Rachel's voice rang out clear and sweet. Then, as the audience applauded, the cousins curtsied with their full skirts. Hannah Elizabeth caught a glimpse of her mother's sur-

prised but pleased face. Mother and Father Shrock, Uncle 'Lijah and Aunt Ellen had known nothing about the Great Debut until this moment.

The curtsying and delicious clapping continued until Cousin Eva explained to the two new stars in the firmament, "They want you to do another song."

"We don't know any other," Hannah Elizabeth said honestly. A ripple of kind amusement flowed over the audience.

Then Rachel moved gracefully across the platform and swept down the wooden steps, her sixteen gores billowing gracefully. Hannah Elizabeth followed with much dignity, holding her head high. She reached the top step.

What a relief! The Great Debut was over! It had been a splendiferous success. Hannah Elizabeth, feeling positively exuberant from all that clapping, jumped down the remaining steps in sheer joy and relief. She wanted to get to her seat as quickly as possible.

Oh, treacherous circumstance! Oh, devastating disaster! How could it ever have happened? Hannah Elizabeth's feet were suddenly where her head should have been. Her right elbow was bruised. Her sixteen-gored skirt was smudged with dirt. She had to pick herself up in front of all those people, and one place where it hurt she could not even rub. The Great Debut had become for Hannah Elizabeth Shrock the Great Debacle.

How did she get to her seat? How did Great-Uncle M.S. close the program? She did not know. Was this not enough? No. Cousin Paul had to admonish her. "Just what you get for acting so smart, Hanny Lizard. Don't you know the Bible says *Pride goeth before a fall?* That was quite a fall too." He laughed and was off to join a group of ballplayers.

Hannah Elizabeth's cheeks burned. She felt mortified, just mortified. Could she ever look at anyone again? Ever, ever, ever in her life. That Paul! How she hated him! Well, not hate, exactly. The Bible said that *whosoever hateth his brother is a murderer.* She was not a murderer. But she certainly did dislike Paul. He'd better not call her Hanny Lizard again either. It would be bad enough to be called Lizzie like the Elizabeth grandmother, now dead, for whom she was named. Hanny Lizard! How unpoetic could you get?

"Hannah Elizabeth," Rachel said in confidential tones.

"Yes?" Perhaps dear Rachel would soothe her deeply ruffled feelings.

"You know what? I really want to be an airplane stewardess when I grow up. And you're the only one in the whole wide world who knows."

"Really?" Hannah Elizabeth's eyes suddenly shone, for she understood the enormity of her cousin's confession.

≫ TWO

Jailbirds and a Poem

Fourth grade for Hannah Elizabeth Shrock had been a distressing wilderness. What would fifth grade and the new teacher, Miss Davis, be like?

To understand why fourth grade had been like a wild raspberry patch in a woods, you must know about two things that happened there.

The First Thing That Happened: Hannah Elizabeth was not allowed to read library books in free time for three months because she was not on the honor roll. She had D's in handwriting. Her writing was so scrawly and messy that the fourth-grade teacher could not give her a higher mark. She was to practice handwriting, instead of reading stories and poems, every school day for a whole month. And this happened three separate months. It was agony, unadulterated agony. Could she help it if she was ugly and her handwriting was ugly? How could she learn to be a poet that way?

The Second Thing That Happened: One day Bruce Brown, Hannah Elizabeth's Liberty neighbor, announced to the entire class, "Hannah's father is a jailbird. He went to jail in the World War because he would not fight." Hannah Elizabeth hung her head. It was true, and she was furious at Bruce for telling. The others in the class—Patricia and Roberta, for example—would simply not understand. Bruce was a neighbor of the Shrocks. He knew that her father was the kindest man in the world. Why did he tell? Jailbirds were murderers and thieves. They were bad. Father Shrock was not that kind of person. But he had been in jail. She blinked back her tears. *Jailbird* was an ugly word. An ugly, ugly word!

The fourth-grade teacher tightened her lips. "This is a free country, Bruce," she said tersely, "and there are some very narrow-minded people in it." She meant the Mennonites. She thought Hannah Elizabeth's family was unpatriotic and did not love the United States of America because her father had not gone into the army. But she steered the class discussion in another direction.

Hannah Elizabeth could not keep her mind on schoolwork. She was thinking about what Bruce had said. She knew why her father had gone to prison. She knew the Scripture verses by heart. They were Jesus's words. *Love your enemies, bless them that curse you, do good to them that hate you, and pray for them that despitefully use you and persecute you.*

It was part of the Mennonite way of life. Christians did not join armies to fight other people. They were to love all people, even their enemies. Even Bruce. *We ought to obey God rather than men,* her father often quoted from the Bible. That is why, long before Hannah

Elizabeth was born, he had once gone to prison rather than into the army. He had felt that he must obey God rather than the government. To Hannah Elizabeth it seemed a brave thing to do, for he had been mistreated by guards, and it was hard to love and pray for those guards.

At recess some of the boys began to chant:
"Her daddy was a jailbird!
Her daddy was a jailbird!"

Hannah Elizabeth winced. If only she could drop into the ground or just melt into the air. If only Rachel went to this school. Rachel might know what to do. *Jailbird!*

"Cut it out, guys!" Bruce Brown himself came to her rescue. "I didn't mean that you should pick on her. She can't help it. Her dad sure seems okay now."

Hannah Elizabeth was grateful to Bruce. He had meant no harm. For the rest of the fourth-graders that ended the incident. Patricia and Roberta had not even noticed. But Hannah Elizabeth did not forget. Did she imagine it, or did the fourth-grade teacher sometimes have little lines of disdain at the edges of her mouth when she looked at Hannah Elizabeth?

During the happy summer days with her family and church friends these two Things That Happened lay deeply buried within Hannah Elizabeth. She did not think of them. She almost forgot the stinging word *jailbird*. Then came September, the opening of school, fifth grade and, above all, Miss Davis.

Hannah Elizabeth adored Miss Davis. Why? Because she was gentle and kind. She loved stories and poems. She knew how to make school fun, even handwriting and arithmetic. And, wonder of wonders, she had faintly purplish freckles on her nose. Hannah Elizabeth hoped fervently that wonderful Miss Davis would never find out that her father had once been in prison. If Miss Davis found out that her father was a jailbird—ugly word!—she might never like her again.

Miss Davis taught the fifth-graders to use the encyclopedia. She had a list entitled "Great Americans" and told her students that when their other work was done, they could choose one of the names, do research on the person, then write and present a report to the class. How exciting! Hannah Elizabeth would do all the poets.

One day Bruce Brown was ready with a report on Henry David Thoreau. Hannah Elizabeth sat back to listen.

"Henry David Thoreau was born at Concord, Massachusetts, on July 12, 1817," Bruce began. He continued reading until he reached the following sentences.

"Once Thoreau was put in jail because he refused to pay his poll tax. He said that because the government supported war and slavery, he could not support the government. While in jail, he wrote his famous . . ."

Here Bruce stopped and looked up with conviction. "I can't understand how this guy Thoreau could have been a great American if he was a jailbird."

Miss Davis smiled. "Bruce, society jails its greatest sinners and its greatest saints. I must

confess that I have ancestors who have been in jail. And I'm proud of them."

What? What? Hannah Elizabeth wriggled. Had she heard correctly? "Its greatest sinners and its greatest saints"?

Miss Davis was speaking again. "My ancestors were British Quakers who knew what the inside of a jail was like. They came to Pennsylvania to find religious freedom. William

Penn invited peace-loving people like the Brethren and the Mennonites"—and here Miss Davis looked straight at Hannah Elizabeth— "to come to Penn's Woods, as his colony was called. Because these people believed in loving all men everywhere, the record of treatment of the Indians was better in Pennsylvania than in any of the twelve other colonies. As you study history, Bruce, you will find that Thoreau is not the only great jailbird. The Apostle Paul in the Bible was one too."

Bruce nodded, shrugged his shoulders and continued his report, but Hannah Elizabeth did not hear a word of it. She was all glad inside. It was as though a piece of the wide Indiana sky were there. *Joyful, Joyful, We Adore Thee!* To Miss Davis it would not matter a bit that her father had once been in jail because he did not believe in war. It might even be a good thing. Miss Davis would understand how much Hannah Elizabeth and her people, the Mennonites, loved a country where they had freedom of conscience.

That afternoon the fifth-graders looked at a poem in their readers.

> It is not growing like a tree
> In bulk, doth make man better be;
> Or standing long an oak, three hundred year,
> To fall a log at last, dry, bald, and sere:
> A lily of a day
> Is fairer far in May
> Although it fall and die that night,
> It was the plant and flower of Light.
> In small proportions we just beauties see,
> And in short measures life may perfect be.

It was the hardest poem Hannah Elizabeth had ever seen. How did you ever figure out things like that? It was like that sentence in the Bible: *There is a river, the streams whereof shall make glad the city of God.* It seemed to say one thing, but it meant a great deal more. If she was ever going to be a poet, she had to understand mysterious words like these.

Miss Davis helped the fifth-graders see that a lily that lasts only a day may be just as beautiful and meaningful as an oak tree that lives three hundred years. The life of a baby that lives only a few months may be as meaningful as the life of a man who lives ninety years. She read the last two lines and commented gently, "Children, the small things that happen make life beautiful." Then she gave them their assignment. "For tomorrow study the poem and write down something you see in it."

Hannah Elizabeth chewed her pencil and puckered her forehead for a long time. At last she wrote in messy, scrawly handwriting:

"When an oak tree gets old and dies, it loses its leaves. It is bald. When a man gets old, he loses his hair and he is bald."

The next day Miss Davis read what she had written. "You have thought of a simile, Hannah Elizabeth. An oak tree is like an old man." Then she added gently, "If you improve your handwriting, I can understand your ideas more easily."

That is how Hannah Elizabeth Shrock came to add "simile" to her vocabulary and how she resolved to improve her handwriting.

❧ THREE

The Diamond and the Gingerbread House

The autumn days slipped softly by like scarlet beads on a silver necklace. A haze of glory covered her little corner of Indiana. The maples were a riot of color over her head and under her feet. Corn shocks marched in straight rows across fields toward husking time.

There is a river, the streams whereof shall make glad . . . make glad . . .

When would she ever find out what those tantalizing words meant?

At home after school each day Hannah Elizabeth quickly did her assigned jobs. Each Wednesday afternoon Mrs. Dargent, the music teacher, came to give her a piano lesson. Mrs. Dargent lived in the big town of Kokomo. Hannah Elizabeth had been to Kokomo with her parents to shop a few times. But she had never visited anyone who lived there.

Sometimes on Wednesday afternoons Hannah Elizabeth looked at Mrs. Dargent and wondered about her as she talked about scales, arpeggios and chords. She had no children. What was her house like? Like old Mrs. Corry's Gingerbread House?

On other days Hannah Elizabeth had an hour to spend or squander entirely as she pleased. Since no other girls lived in Liberty, Hannah Elizabeth had to play with the boys or make her own play. One afternoon she headed for the pasture diamond where the boys met. A baseball game was in full swing. Hannah Elizabeth hung around the edges for a while. She wanted to play but was too shy to ask. And her pride was involved. They should ask her.

She knew she was a miserable baseball player. But it was no fun just to stand there.

At last Bruce Brown called out gallantly but reluctantly, "You can be on our side, Hannah Liz."

Did she imagine that the other fellows on Bruce's team were groaning inwardly but were too nice to show it? The boys knew that whenever it was her turn to bat, her team automatically had an out.

Well, she would hit that ball today for a change. She would. She would show them. She would.

When it was her turn, she held the bat desperately, tensed her muscles and tried hard to swing it correctly. It went in amazing directions. Chop! Flop!

"Strike one!" the umpire yelled. "Right over the plate."

Maybe she had not watched the ball carefully enough to see where it was when it was coming. Next time she concentrated on the ball.

"Strike two. Right over the plate."

33 ✒

Dear, oh, dear! She had forgotten to move the bat in time.

Charlie, the pitcher, was almost as desperate as she was. "Just hold your bat out straight and let me hit it," he suggested.

Even that was not easy for Hannah Elizabeth. The bat was heavy. Charlie aimed carefully and hit the bat, and the ball bounced a few feet back into the diamond. But Hannah Elizabeth did not reach first base before the ball did. It was an uneven match—her two legs moving up and down on the ground versus a legless ball whizzing through the air from the catcher to the sure hands of the first baseman.

This was terrible. Just terrible. It was so easy for the rest of them.

"I know what!" Bruce finally suggested with a flash of inspiration. "You can be scorekeeper, Hannah Liz. You can keep track of the hits, runs and errors."

Errors? Those would be mistakes, of course. What kind of mistakes? She asked aloud, "What's the difference between a hit and a run?"

Now Bruce was getting desperate. "Oh, for cat's sake, Hanny Lizard, just keep track of how many runs each side gets. You know what that is, don't you?"

She knew what that was. Hanny Lizard! Grrrr! Bruce was as unpoetic as Cousin Paul. She also knew when she was not wanted. She should have gone to the Gingerbread House instead of coming to the diamond. Hannah Elizabeth mustered just as much dignity as she could under the circumstances and said clearly, "I have to go home now because we may be getting company." No one paid the slightest attention to her. Bruce had just hit a homer.

"It's a silly game," Hannah Elizabeth thought scornfully as she headed toward Mrs. Corry's little brown house. "Knocking a ball around with a stick of wood!" Nevertheless, she was wounded in spirit.

Hannah Elizabeth felt a twinge of conscience about having said they might be getting company. The Bible said, *Speak the truth to thy neighbor, and lie not.* But they *might* be getting company. She didn't know. You never could tell. And she did have to go home—after a while. She wondered whether God understood how it felt to be such a poor ballplayer. Probably not. He could do anything. It was awful to be ugly and not know how to hit a ball with a bat.

Hannah Elizabeth's feet took her down Mrs. Corry's brick-lined sidewalk, past zinnia beds and geraniums to the porch. She never mentioned to anyone that she always called Mrs. Corry's house the Gingerbread House in her mind because, with its crumbly-looking turret, its spire and its spicy brown windows, it looked like the witch's house in "Hansel and Gretel."

Mrs. Corry, as unlike a witch as anyone could be, met her at the door. "Come in, little Hannah Elizabeth," she said heartily, all the wrinkles in her face smiling. "I'm so glad you came." Hannah Elizabeth breathed deeply and noted with satisfaction that here she was appreciated. "I'm just finishing apples for sauce. Let's go into the living room and visit awhile."

"Oh, no. Let's stay in the kitchen. I'll help

you," Hannah Elizabeth answered. That is what Mother would have said.

Mrs. Corry obligingly gave her a pan of apples and a knife. She also gave her a thick sour-cream cookie. "You don't have to peel the apples. I'll run them through the colander. Just cut them into four pieces and take out the core. You have to watch for wormy spots in some of them.

"I remember when I was young . . ." Mrs. Corry began, and with these familiar words she was off into one of her stories. "I remember when I was young, we used to cook apple butter in a big copper kettle over an open fire. Your folks still do."

Hannah Elizabeth nodded. She knew all about cooking "lodvike." Grandfather and Grandmother Shrock always asked their family to help at apple-butter time every fall.

"You know, I think apple butter cooked in a big kettle over an open fire tastes better than that made in little dabs on top of a stove," Mrs. Corry declared. "I believe it does. We all had

to take turns at the big wooden paddle. Stirring the apple butter so's it wouldn't get stuck at the bottom and burn, you know. The burn would taste through a whole batch."

"I suppose so," Hannah Elizabeth observed.

"When I worked for old Elias Deeterbaugh, it was always my job to wash the wooden apple-butter paddle. And I can tell you, if it wasn't soaked, that dried-on apple butter was hard to get off!" Mrs. Corry laughed a merry laugh.

Hannah Elizabeth nodded soberly. "I suppose it was."

"I always liked to lick the wooden paddle as soon as it had cooled off enough. But old Mrs. Deeterbaugh—Armintha Deeterbaugh, Mintie they called her—was a strict woman. She caught me at it once and gave me Hail Columbia." Mrs. Corry laughed heartily at the long-ago incident. "I said to her, 'Listen here, Mintie Deeterbaugh, someday I'm going to grow up and lick my own apple-butter paddle.' I never have, though," Mrs. Corry concluded a little sadly before taking off in another direction.

"Mintie Deeterbaugh was a Democrat, you know."

Hannah Elizabeth shook her head. She had never heard of Mintie Deeterbaugh until today. Mintie had probably been dead for fifty years. How could Hannah Elizabeth possibly know about her politics?

"Oh, yes. She was a Democrat. Her husband and six sons were all Republicans. Once the Republicans had a rally over here at the Chestnut Creek School. While they were having their speeches and all, what did that woman do but take a hammer and nail a picture of the Democratic candidate right onto the schoolhouse door!" Mrs. Corry chuckled. "Oh, I tell you, she was a character, that Armintha Deeterbaugh."

Hannah Elizabeth supposed she was.

"Longer ago we had more corn-huskings and barn-raisings and such like. It wasn't just your people that did it. It was everybody. Why I remember the night your grandpa—no, it was your great-grandpa! How time does fly! I remember the night your Great-Grandpa Simon Shrock and Great-Grandma Caroline Troyer started going together."

"You do!" Hannah Elizabeth sat on the edge of her kitchen stool, water dripping down her elbows. She tried to push her mind back into the darkness of time that had existed before she was born, before her father and mother were born, and even before her grandfather and grandmother were born. It was a strenuous activity, like trying to see into very Dark Ages.

"We were having a log-burning over here at the Silas Kaser place. You know, this county was all swampland at one time. I've often heard the older folks tell of how they had to dig ditches and clear the land before they could do any cultivating."

Hannah Elizabeth was not getting many apples cored. She kept jabbing the knife into her thumb. Would Mrs. Corry never get to the part about Great-Grandfather and Great-Grandmother?

"You started to tell me about my Great—"

"Oh, yes. Well, all the girls thought Simon Shrock was just the nicest young man for miles around. He was strong and handsome. The older girls all sort of had their eyes on him—I was young then." Mrs. Corry chuckled. "Caroline Troyer—your great-grandmother, you know . . ."

Hannah Elizabeth nodded.

"Caroline Troyer was so bashful and shy— not a bit forward, you know—that we thought none of the young fellows even knew she was around. We girls all kind of stood and waited to see who the young fellows would ask. And that night, if Simon Shrock didn't walk right up and tell Caroline Troyer he'd walk her home if she'd let him."

Hannah Elizabeth did not see the wormholes in the apples. She forgot all about her recent hurts at the Liberty baseball diamond. This story was like a thunderbolt. Hannah Elizabeth shivered with excitement as she thought of it.

If Great-Grandmother Caroline had said no to Great-Grandfather Simon, then they would not have married. If Great-Grandfather Simon had not married Great-Grandmother Caroline, then Grandfather Joseph would never have been born. If Grandfather Joseph had not married Grandmother Hannah, then Father Mark would never have been born. If Father Mark had not married Mother Susan, then Hannah Elizabeth would never have been born.

She saw that she was alive because of a long chain of events. If any one link in the chain had not been hooked onto the previous link, she, Hannah Elizabeth Shrock, ten years old, sitting here in the Gingerbread House, would not exist at all. She would not be alive and peeling apples for Mrs. Corry. She was alive because Great-Grandmother Caroline had said yes instead of no at a long-ago log burning. What a narrow escape!

"Mother says Hanny Lizbeth is supposed to come right away and set the table." Timothy Joseph was at the screen door of Mrs. Corry's kitchen with a kitten under each arm. "Besides," he added, "we have company. Grandpa and Grandma are there."

Hannah Elizabeth felt relieved. She had not

told those baseball boys a lie after all. They did have company.

"Come back again," Mrs. Corry told her, at the same time giving a cookie to Tim. "I'm always glad to have you."

At home Hannah Elizabeth looked at her grandparents with wide eyes. How precious they were! Did Grandfather realize that he would not exist if Great-Grandmother Caroline had said no to Great-Grandfather Simon at that log-burning? Probably not. He acted calm as could be. Hannah Elizabeth wanted to hug her grandparents with all her might. It seemed she had come so close to losing them in the Gingerbread House. But hugging and kissing were not the custom in the Shrock family. She greeted them politely: "Hello."

Grandfather and Grandmother had come to get the quilt frames and the outdoor copper kettle which Hannah Elizabeth's family had borrowed. Grandfather and Grandmother owned these items, but the families of the six sons and six daughters, all except missionary Uncle Daniel's in India, also used them.

"We'll cook apple butter next Tuesday afternoon," Grandfather said to Mother.

"Could Mrs. Corry come too?" Hannah Elizabeth asked eagerly.

"A good idea," Mother said. "I think she would enjoy helping cook apple butter once again."

"And perhaps she could lick the wooden paddle when we're through," Hannah Elizabeth suggested.

"She'd be welcome to," Grandmother said with surprise. "But I can't imagine why a woman her age would want to lick an apple-butter paddle."

Hannah Elizabeth set the table. She just had to say one more thing. At last a big enough gap occurred in the conversation. "Isn't it a good thing we have ancestors!"

Mother looked startled. Grandmother's eyes danced. Grandfather said warmly, "It is indeed, little Hannah Elizabeth. We enjoy water because of a well Father Jacob dug."

Although Hannah Elizabeth did not understand Grandfather's words, she did understand the way he said them, and the river that made things glad seemed somehow to be flowing from Jacob's well.

Mrs. Corry did indeed lick the apple-butter paddle the next week and enjoyed every minute of it.

FOUR

The Trees Choose a King

One glorious autumn afternoon Hannah Elizabeth got off the orange school bus (called the "school hack" in her community) at the end of Grandfather Shrock's long lane. She carried a book Miss Davis had lent her, *Fairy Tales* by Hans Christian Andersen. Grandfather Shrock's lane seemed somehow to separate Hannah Elizabeth's school world from her Mennonite world.

Sometimes the two worlds bumped into each other confusingly. Grandfather, for instance. There he was now, whistling merrily and mending fence along one side of the lane. He wore faded blue overalls and a battered straw hat. At school he would have looked wrong. Ministers were not to look like Grandfather looked. They were to wear dress suits every day of the week and to have been to college and seminary.

"Little Hannah Elizabeth!" Grandfather called out to her. "Welcome!"

"Mother said I could stay here and go to church with you tonight," Hannah Elizabeth explained. "It's just a beatific day, isn't it, Grandfather?"

Grandfather laughed, but he was not laughing at her. "It's only a faint shadow of all the glory that is to come, little granddaughter. *Here we have no continuing city, but we seek one to come.*"

Here was a city again. Was it the same city that the river made glad? What was Grandfather talking about? Hannah Elizabeth did not know, but she loved the comradeship of being treated as an equal, and the words stuck in her mind like burs on a coat.

Just then who should come riding down the lane on his bicycle but Cousin Paul. "Hi, Hanny! Hi, Grandpa!" Paul would not dare call her "Hanny Lizard" in Grandfather's presence. He skidded to a stop and propped the stand under his bike. "Father sent me to help you chore because it's church night," he explained to Grandfather. Grandfather and sometimes Grandmother milked eight cows every morning and evening.

At home in Liberty Mother or Father always milked their one cow, but Hannah Elizabeth had watched them often enough. She could probably milk a cow.

"I'll be glad to help too," she volunteered. She could be just as helpful as Paul.

Grandfather was a minister, but he was also a farmer. Long before Hannah Elizabeth or Paul or Rachel or any of the other grandchildren were born, Grandfather had become a minister in the following way. His fellow church members had chosen him and several other devout men to go into the "lot." That is, in a solemn religious service each one of them chose a hymnbook. In one of these books was a slip of paper on which was written a Scripture reference. Grandfather's book contained that paper. From that day on he had continued farming, but a heavy burden of preaching and leadership had also rested upon his shoulders.

Paul was already unwinding a coil of wire for Grandfather. He was a good worker and saw immediately what to do.

Hannah Elizabeth started toward the house. Fence-mending she would not attempt. "Tell Grandmother we'll be ready to chore in a half hour," Grandfather called after her.

Grandmother had just finished making sauerkraut in the summerhouse, sometimes called "the little house." It was the building in which many of Grandfather's twelve children had begun housekeeping and to which the grandparents would move when they wished to retire and turn the farm over to one of their children.

Hannah Elizabeth delivered the message to Grandmother. She put *Fairy Tales* with the

Gospel Herald, the church paper, on the dining-
room table. Soon the four of them, Grandfather
and Grandmother Shrock, Paul and Hannah
Elizabeth, were in the cow barn getting organ-
ized for the job of milking.

"Buttercup has been balky lately," Grandfather commented.

"Let me milk her. She'll be okay for me,"

Paul said confidently. He knew all about cows and milking. He put hobbles on Buttercup's hind legs to keep her from kicking. Soon the milk was streaming rhythmically into his empty milk bucket.

Zing-zang. Zing-zang.
Zing-zang. Zing-zang.

"Suppose you try Dolly, Hannah Elizabeth," Grandmother suggested. "She's our gentlest cow." Grandfather and Grandmother Shrock had so many grandchildren that they did not know which ones could milk cows and which could not.

Hannah Elizabeth sat down to Dolly. She carefully placed the milk bucket under the big udder. By now the milk streams into the other three pails were zinging and zanging in various rhythms.

Hannah Elizabeth took Dolly's two front teats in her right and left hands. She squeezed. She squeezed. Nothing happened. Dolly stood there placidly munching hay. What if she kicked? Hannah Elizabeth did not know how to fasten hobbles.

Paul saw her predicament and came over to help her. "Look! It's simple," he said. "Use the ball part of your four fingers. Squeeze the center of the teat from top to bottom against the other side of your hand. Like this!"

Squirt. Squirt. The milk streamed easily into the bucket. Paul went back to Buttercup. Hannah Elizabeth tried again. She tried so hard that she was blinking back tears. This was terrible. Just terrible. Whatever could she do? She sniffed and got up resolutely. Cows were totally uninteresting creatures.

"Grandmother, I'm going to the house to get supper ready," she said.

Grandmother looked somewhat surprised. "That's fine. The apple-butter dish needs filling from the crock in the cellar. And you can peel the potatoes."

Paul looked at Hannah Elizabeth pityingly as she left the barn. He did not say a word, but she could almost read his thoughts: "Gee whiz! Can't even milk a cow."

Inside the quiet house Hannah Elizabeth breathed deeply. She was glad to be away from the smelly cow stable. What a delicious feeling it was to be all alone in Grandfather's house. At home and school there were always other people around. Her soul seemed to grow best when she was not talking or listening to out-loud talk.

First she got the everyday dishes from the cupboard. Grandmother's dishes were white with little orange-breasted bluebirds on them. Hannah Elizabeth thought they looked like the happiest dishes in the world. She set four places instead of the six she usually set at home. Paul would probably stay for supper. Mother used oilcloth on their table at home in Liberty because of the inevitable drops and spills. Grandmother used a blue-and-tan plaid linen cloth, just the right background for the bluebird dishes.

Hannah Elizabeth washed and sliced tomatoes and sprinkled salt on them. She peeled potatoes and left them standing in a pan of cold water all ready for Grandmother to slice for frying. She filled the apple-butter dish. She put homemade bread on the wooden breadboard and laid the bread knife beside them on the table. She sliced home-cured ham, cutting her left index finger in the process. Then she stepped back to survey her work and decided that it was good.

Now she had time to put a few stitches in Grandmother's flower-garden quilt. No. She might stick her finger with the needle and make a blood stain on the quilt. She would read until the others came in.

Hannah Elizabeth curled up on a rocker near the dining-room window with the book Miss Davis had lent her. Soon she was deeply absorbed. Grandmother's corner cupboard filled with heirloom dishes, the fronded fern, the comfortable rocker—all faded away. On this evening, for the first time in her life, Hannah Elizabeth Shrock met someone she understood completely. His name was the Ugly Duckling.

It was terrible the way all the barnyard fowls pecked at him. How lonely he was. He hated being homely and different. Why couldn't he be just like the others? How could he help being what he was? And that horrid hen and cat who asked with such devastating logic, "Can you lay eggs? Can you arch your back, purr or give off sparks?" Of course he couldn't. Hannah Elizabeth shrank inside. Can you write neatly? Can you hit a baseball with a bat? Can't you even milk a cow?

Then came the beautiful birds flying high, high in the sky and the piercing longing. Oh, he was a swan all the time! The Ugly Duckling was really a swan, the most beautiful swan of them all! He was a swan. Oh, almost unbearable joy!

"You'll ruin your eyes reading in such poor light." Grandmother brought Hannah Elizabeth from her book back to the dining room. The hum of the separator began in the cellar under the kitchen, where Grandfather and Paul were separating the milk.

Grandmother surveyed her kitchen. "Everything is all neat and ready. You are a good cook, little Hannah. Ay! Ay! And you've even sliced the ham!"

Hannah Elizabeth closed her book with a sigh. Grandmother had called her a good cook. She had helped almost as much as Paul. She hid her cut finger and felt happy.

At church that night Rachel and Hannah Elizabeth were not interested in Uncle Paton's report of a conference on mutual aid. Church representatives were always going to conferences on dull-sounding subjects. Nor were they interested in the meeting topic, "Bringing Up Children in the Fear of the Lord." The girls settled down on the third bench in the meeting-house and began to play a hymnbook game they had invented. Hannah Elizabeth pricked up her ears, however, when she heard Uncle Moses ask in the grownup discussion, "Should you ever tell children stories that are not true?"

Great-Uncle Ananias rose to speak. "I may be mistaken. They're still putting erasers on lead pencils, you know." He chuckled. Genial Great-Uncle Ananias often prefaced meeting remarks with that statement. Then he became serious. "I believe we should not tell children stories that are not true. Doesn't the Bible say in Proverbs that the Lord hates a heart that devises wicked imaginations?"

He sat down, and Brother Jacob rose to his feet. Brother Jacob, a co-minister with Grand-

father, was one of the few old men in the congregation who still had beards. Hannah Elizabeth loved to watch it bobbing up and down, snow-white, soft and silky, when he talked. "I wish to say yea and amen to all that Brother Ananias has just said," he began. "In some stories animals are made to talk. Yet we all know, beloved brothers and sisters, that animals do not talk. Such vain imagination is surely the work of the Evil One. We need to be on guard, beloved, lest we corrupt the most precious possession the Lord has entrusted to us—namely, our children." Brother Jacob sat down.

Hannah Elizabeth looked around with alarm. Would no one speak for the Ugly Duckling, Hansel and Gretel and the thousand dear characters alive forever in the stories she loved?

"I once made up a story to teach my children to obey." It was Mother's voice. She did not often speak in church, and she did not stand now because little Aaron was asleep on her lap. The hymnbook game was quite forgotten.

"Maybe stories that didn't really happen are truer in a way than those that did. Isn't it perfectly all right to tell them to children?" Mother finished gently and without much logic, but with conviction in her voice.

Great-Aunt Katie spoke next. "I know Sister Susan means well, but aren't there enough good true stories in the world to tell to children? Why do we have to make up any more?"

The meeting fell into silence. Mother's honor, Hans Christian Andersen, Hannah Elizabeth's magic hours of reading, all seemed to be sinking into a deep black hole.

Then Grandfather Shrock stood and read without comment from his Bible:

> *The trees went forth on time*
> *To anoint a king over them;*
> *And they said unto the olive tree:*
> *Reign thou over us!*
> *But the olive tree said unto them:*
> *Should I leave my fatness,*
> *Wherewith by me they honour God and man,*
> *And go to be promoted over the trees?*
> *And the trees said to the fig tree:*

Come thou, and reign over us!
But the fig tree said unto them:
  Should I forsake my sweetness,
  And my good fruit,
  And go to be promoted over the trees?
Then said the trees unto the vine:
  Come thou, and reign over us!
And the vine said unto them:
  Should I leave my wine,
  Which cheereth God and man,
  And go to be promoted over the trees?
Then said all the trees unto the bramble:
  Come thou, and reign over us!
And the bramble said unto the trees:
  If in truth ye anoint me king over you,
  Then come and put your trust in my shadow;
  And if not, let fire come out of the bramble,
  And devour the cedars of Lebanon.

—JUDGES 9:8–15

Grandfather sat down. Everyone knew that if it was in the Bible, it had to be all right. A rush of love and gratitude for Grandfather filled Hannah Elizabeth. Mother, Hans Christian Andersen and all the world's storytellers had just been vindicated in the Mennonite meeting.

Christmas at Two Ends of the Lane

Halloween and Thanksgiving came and went. One morning Hannah Elizabeth turned the kitchen calendar. December. Christmas was on the way.

"A letter came for you," Mother said to her that afternoon after school.

The white envelope was addressed in red ink with a flourishing hand to

> Miss Hannah E. Shrock
> Rural Route 1
> Liberty, Indiana

What could it be? The "Miss" and the middle initial made it seem quite grownup, and few things in the world hold more possibilities than an unopened letter.

Hannah Elizabeth clumsily slid her finger under the flap of the envelope. Inside was a correspondence folder with a green sequin-decorated Christmas tree on it. Inside the folder were these words written in red ink:

> You and your parents are invited to meet at our apartment, 711 Willow St. West, Friday afternoon, Dec. 21 at 2:30 to attend a matinee followed by a Christmas party.

R.S.V.P.   Mr. and Mrs. Claude Dargent

A Christmas party! What could be more exciting! To think of getting to visit Mrs. Dargent's home! Hannah Elizabeth became a blob of anticipation.

"Oh, please, may I go, Mother?"

Mother frowned. "How would you get there? Your father will be working all day. It's fifteen miles to town." Then, seeing the quick cloud cross her daughter's face, she added gently, "We'll see. Perhaps you can go with

Bruce Brown and his parents. Do try not to get so excited about things. Do you know what a matinee is?"

Hannah Elizabeth did not know. She was too close to tears and too proud to admit it. Secretly she looked it up in her old dictionary. When would she get a new one? "A musical or dramatic entertainment held in the daytime, esp. in the afternoon." She looked up R.S.V.P. in the abbreviation section and found it meant *Répondez, s'il vous plaît,* French for please reply.

If a matinee was what the girls at school called an "afternoon show," maybe Mother and Father would not let her go. In Hannah Elizabeth's community Mennonites did not go to movies. They quoted from the Bible: *Whatsoever things are true, whatsoever things are honest, whatsoever things are just, whatsoever things are pure, whatsoever things are lovely, whatsoever things are of good report; if there be any virtue, and if there be any praise, think on these things.* They said you could tell by the newspaper and billboard advertisements alone that movies were not true, honest, just, pure, lovely and of good report. So why go?

But if your piano teacher sent you a lovely Christmas invitation written in red ink, and if there was to be a party with decoration, games, prizes, refreshments! Hannah Elizabeth could not bear to think of not going.

The next afternoon she said to Mother, "The R.S.V.P. means that I should reply to Mrs. Dargent's invitation."

"I know," Mother replied. "Bruce Brown's mother told me today that you could go with them." She paused a little. "Do you really want to go?"

Hannah Elizabeth understood the pause. Mother respected her freedom to choose whether to be a good Mennonite or not.

"Yes, I do, Mother."

Under Mother's direction Hannah Elizabeth wrote the reply. She composed it on brown wrapping paper, for Mother Shrock was well aware of the smudgy, messy writing and did not believe in wasting good white paper. After all the revisions were made, Hannah Elizabeth copied the final words onto a sheet of her own stationery.

> Dear Mr. and Mrs. Dargent,
>   I shall be happy to accept your kind invitation for December 21. Thank you. My parents will be unable to come.
>
>   Sincerely,
>   Hannah Elizabeth Shrock

The last sentence was true really. Father had to work, as usual. Mother could not drive a car. And someone had to stay with Timothy, Thomas and Aaron. Yet Hannah Elizabeth knew that her parents would not have gone even if circumstances had permitted, and she was boundlessly grateful that she did not have to write, "My parents do not wish to come."

"What would you like to take as a present to Mrs. Dargent?" Mother asked Hannah Elizabeth.

"I don't know. I hadn't thought of it. What could I take?"

"I could make her an apron," Mother suggested.

Aprons seemed terribly prosaic to Hannah Elizabeth. It was all right to give aprons to Mrs. Corry for her birthday and Christmas. But she could not imagine that music teachers or people like Miss Davis ever wore them. "Couldn't I take something else?"

"What about several jars of strawberry preserves and some Christmas cookies?" This suggestion was acceptable to Hannah.

One morning Father said to Mother, "Even the smallest Christmas trees cost seventy-five cents." They were talking Pennsylvania Dutch, as they did when they did not want their children to understand them, but Hannah Elizabeth understood every word, although she never let them know she did.

"I don't see how we can afford it this year," Mother replied. "Perhaps we could use a branch from one of our own trees."

That night Father brought into the house a limb he had chopped from one of their cherry

trees. "Here's our tree," he announced. Hannah Elizabeth and her brothers were puzzled. Of course it was a tree—part of one, at least. Mother soon had them busy finding out what he meant.

First they wrapped the gray winter branches with green crepe paper. Mother popped corn and soon had Hannah Elizabeth stringing it up with a needle, a job at which she twisted her tongue and lips as much as her fingers. The little boys were busy with crayons, transforming strips of white wrapping paper into bright red, green, purple and orange chain links. Father nailed the cherry limb to two crossed pieces of wood and put it on a table near a window. Then he carefully split English walnuts —a gift from his employer—removed the nut meats and glued the shell halves together with a loop of string at the end. Together the family traced on red and blue paper a bird pattern Father had drawn. They cut out the paper birds, folded them, drew in eyes and beaks with black crayon, and tied cardinals and bluebirds to the tree branches with pieces of yarn.

Mother poured steaming syrup over a dishpanful of huge yellow popcorn kernels. As soon as the sticky mass was cool enough to work, she greased her hands with homemade butter and deftly shaped it into balls. These would be wrapped in scraps of colored cellophane and tied to the branches.

The completed tree was a masterpiece of ingenuity and a joy to behold. Birds sang on its branches. A foil star crowned its tip. And under the tree four crooked little woolen sheep, made from leftover ends of a comforter batt, peeked into a handmade crib that held a tiny cloth Christ Child.

Hannah Elizabeth thought her littlest brother Aaron's sheep looked misshapen indeed, but Mother mentioned specifically that she thought it an especially charming little lamb. So Hannah Elizabeth kept her observation to herself.

Poets and storytellers added their enchantment to Hannah Elizabeth's Christmas. Sometimes her father told them a story after the evening meal. More often her mother did. Hannah Elizabeth liked the one about a poor French girl who set out her tiny wooden sabot on Christmas Eve and found in it next morning a tiny trembling bird. "It would be dreadful to be poor!" Hannah Elizabeth thought with a sigh.

Her mother told of a night when the Christ Child Himself wandered about over the earth on Christmas Eve disguised as a poor waif, trying to find a place to warm Himself. He looked through the windows of great mansions at the festivities and merrymaking there. None of them had room for a ragged begging boy on Christmas Eve. It was a poor widow who invited Him into her cottage to eat hot soup and receive her warm hospitality. Her cottage glowed with a strange, marvelous light that Christmas Eve.

"If the Christ Child came to our house, we would surely take Him in!" thought Hannah Elizabeth, looking at Mother and Father. They would never turn anyone away. The most wonderful things happened in stories, and real life was often so dull. The Christ Child never came to people's houses anymore and asked to be let in. Or did he?

School in Miss Davis's room was as full of good things as Christmas packages, but somewhere there was time for Hannah Elizabeth to count the days until the twenty-first. By now it had grown to the size of Christmas morning itself.

Noon of the day arrived.

Mother inspected Hannah Elizabeth's ears and elbows. She need not have bothered. They were as clean as Grandmother Shrock's freshly scrubbed kitchen. How Hannah Elizabeth wished she could brush her teeth with real toothpaste on occasions like this! She put on her best blue dress, the one with puffed sleeves, a flared skirt and a wide sash. Mother tied big blue ribbons to the ends of her braids.

Hannah Elizabeth began to wrap each bell-, star-, and tree-shaped sugar cookie, the gift to Mrs. Dargent, in wax paper, but her hands were too trembly. In order to keep the cookies from becoming crumbs, Mother took over this job and sent Hannah to the piano, where music, temporarily at least, exercised its age-old power to soothe a savage breast.

Mother packed the cookies in an empty shoebox and wrapped it in red tissue paper that had been used on a present to her the year before. Then she put the shoebox and two glasses of strawberry preserves into a brown grocery bag, added a thick slice of home-smoked ham wrapped in several thicknesses of wax paper and newspaper, and tied a big red ribbon around the top of the brown bag.

"Hold the sack on the bottom," she cautioned Hannah Elizabeth when the Browns drove up.

Hannah Elizabeth could not have felt any more foreign in the middle of Arabia than she did in the theater fifteen miles from her home. Walking itself seemed difficult to her in this strange half-light until she discovered that the floor sloped down. She tried to stay as close as possible to Bruce and his mother and to do exactly as they did. Her stomach pressed up into her lungs and made breathing more difficult than usual. Everyone else seemed completely sure and at ease. What if she made a terrible mistake!

What a relief it was to sit solid on a turned-down folding seat and collect herself before she was hurled down the Alps on skis via newsreel. The movie was a comedy. Two men got into and out of scrapes. When one threw a custard pie into the other's face, the audience roared as

Hannah Elizabeth winced. It did not seem funny to her. She tried to laugh. She was in Rome and wanted desperately to do whatever was proper for Romans to do. She was not being a good Mennonite, and she knew it. It was distinctly uncomfortable.

Hannah Elizabeth did not feel like her normal self until she got out onto the sidewalk, breathed cold, fresh air and saw snow falling through the early winter dusk. Again she had barely collected herself when her feet sank into the carpet of the Dargent apartment. Was she walking on air or feathers? Everything seemed lush and plush—the cushions, the draperies, the grass-topped coffee table, the lampshades. She caught her breath at an evergreen reaching from floor to ceiling, its branches covered with great glass balls, angel hair and bubbly electric lights. Under it were mountains of beautifully decorated packages.

Hannah Elizabeth's brown grocery bag among all that ribbon and holly looked like the ugliest duckling that had ever set foot in any barnyard. Suddenly she was fiercely ashamed. She saw for the first time through someone else's eyes the hand-braided rag carpets, the homemade furniture, the cherry-limb tree and all the plainness of her own home.

At mealtime Hannah Elizabeth had difficulty following the table conversation. Bruce Brown's father said, "Hannah Betsey is awfully serious. Let's make her laugh. Let's keep her from getting as narrow-minded as the rest of her folks."

Hannah Elizabeth blushed and stared down at the Santa Claus napkin in her lap. She felt puzzled and confused and annoyed.

Bruce's mother put a restraining hand on her husband's arm and said, "Now, Howard."

Hannah Elizabeth tried to participate in the laughter, but, as in the movie, the jokes did not seem funny. Inside she was thinking about "narrow-minded." Mr. Brown evidently wanted her to be wide-minded—like he was. Was Mr. Brown wide-minded? She puckered her forehead.

After the meal the six young guests of honor played "pin-the-star-on-the-tree" and a simple card game. Hannah Elizabeth knew she should not play cards. But she had already gone to a movie. Cardboard cards could surely not be any more wicked than Chinese checkers and dominoes, which she had played with her parents and friends many times.

During the first round she concentrated on the rules. During the second round she had a wonderful time. She was winning. "Look at the little card shark!" Bruce's father announced gaily and loudly to the whole company. "If her Grandfather Shrock could only see her now! Wouldn't he hit the ceiling!"

Grandfather! The lovely room spun around a time or two. Why bring Grandfather into this? Suddenly Hannah Elizabeth felt so angry at Mr. Brown that she could have cheerfully pummeled his head with her fists, not that it would have made much of an impression, for her fists were small, soft and unused. Wideminded! Why, Mr. Brown's mind was so small that he thought he knew what Grandfather would think, and he didn't even know Grandfather! Hannah Elizabeth hated Mr. Brown vehemently, and in the same moment she knew that her hatred would be far more displeasing to Grandfather than playing with pieces of cardboard. But the card game was no longer any fun at all.

At gift-unwrapping time Hannah Elizabeth felt her cheeks getting hotter and hotter. Mrs. Dargent unwrapped a box of frilly handkerchiefs, a lavender perfume atomizer, a necklace, a box of bath crystals. Inevitably she would get to the brown paper bag. What if the ham had made a grease spot on the carpet? What if she had brought an apron?

Hannah Elizabeth's mother owned no cosmetics or jewelry of any kind. Hannah Elizabeth had heard over and over the quotations, *"Whose adorning let it not be that outward adorning of plaiting the hair, and of wearing of gold, or of putting on of apparel; but let it be the hidden man of the heart . . . even the orna-*

ment of a meek and quiet spirit." You never bought anything at a dime store to polish up a meek and quiet spirit. Oh, the horror of being the victim of such gross ignorance! To give ham, cookies and preserves to your music teacher as a Christmas gift!

Here I am, beautiful birds. He bowed his head. Peck me to death. I am ugly and ungainly.

Mrs. Dargent slipped the red ribbon from the grocery bag. "Strawberry jam! Home-baked Christmas cookies! Country ham! Oh, thank you, Hannah Elizabeth!" Her voice was warm, genuine.

"Does your father cure his own ham?" Mr. Dargent wanted to know.

Hannah Elizabeth blushed. "Yes, he uses hickory smoke," she stammered.

"Imagine that, Margie!" Mr. Dargent beamed at his wife. "We'll have real hickory-smoked ham for breakfast on Christmas morning."

Bruce Brown's father slapped Mr. Dargent on the back and said, "Doggone it! I wish my wife gave music lessons."

Hannah Elizabeth looked hard at the Dargents. They were not making fun of her. They were not teasing her. They meant every word of it.

Next morning Mother Shrock asked, "Did you have a good time at the party?"

Hannah Elizabeth thought a minute. "Yes and no," she said.

On Christmas Day all but one of Grandfather and Grandmother Shrock's twelve children and their large families drove down the snowy lane to Grandfather's house. Uncle Daniel and his family could not be there, for Uncle Daniel was a medical missionary to India.

The walls of Grandfather's house did not bulge and collapse. The table legs did not bend and break. No one's eardrums burst. But a stranger might have expected any one of these things to happen at any minute. No wonder it had been a treat for Hannah Elizabeth to be alone in that house when she met the Ugly Duckling.

Hannah Elizabeth and Rachel had not eaten so much since Shrock Reunion Day. They carefully avoided the kitchen during dishwashing, and their mothers did not even notice. The two cousins found an upstairs room where there was a little privacy and shared all the secrets they had collected since they were last together.

Cousin Paul helped Uncle Moses hitch a horse to a sleigh. They gave everyone jolly rides. Even fat Aunt Sarah piled in and shouted between laughy shrieks, "Now, Moses, don't go so fast! Don't go so fast! I'm not young anymore. You know I'm not young anymore!"

The uncles and aunts standing on the sidelines laughed and shouted to her in Pennsylvania Dutch, "Are you still a back-seat driver, Sarah?" "Remember when the buggy landed in the strawstack!" Hannah Elizabeth tried to imagine a time when her uncles and aunts were young, but it was hard.

When Aunt Sarah got out of the sleigh, her husband, Uncle Andy, said, "Why, Sarah, that's good for you. You don't look a day over sixteen!" He smacked two kisses on her rosy cheeks right in front of everyone, and for once

Aunt Sarah could not think of a thing to say.

Inside the house various aunts started passing Christmas candies—nut loaf, chocolate fudge, creamy divinity, peanut brittle. Everyone said, "I don't have room for another bite," but they did. The aunts compared recipes.

Soon the uncles and aunts began to tell stories about Christmases of their childhood. Hannah Elizabeth sat on the floor and listened with ears unstopped. Then Grandfather said he wanted to read Uncle Daniel's letter. Everyone became quiet, listening.

Dear ones at home,

Thousands of miles will separate us on the blessed day of our Savior's birth. As I write I stop to wipe beads of perspiration from my forehead. You are no doubt shoveling snow. Yet our thoughts and prayers will be with you at the old homestead on Christmas Day.

Together we will cross Judean hills to Bethlehem and kneel in wonder at its manger. Yes, verily, yes, let us rise up and go even unto Bethlehem. Let us take a long look at this

"thing that is come to pass." Let us ponder
with Mary the deep meanings in our hearts as
we share the Lord's birth.

We rejoice that the work here prospers.
We have two clinics in outlying villages. The
home for lepers is growing. We badly need
another sterilizer and a second refrigerator for
the hospital.

Elnora is starting a school for the children
of lepers. These children are no more diseased
than yours and ours. Yet they bear a stigma
because of their parents. No one wishes to

care for them, and often their own parents cannot.

Just now one of these children, seven-year-old Ramsilla, is living with us. She has gained weight since she came, and she is rapidly learning to read. Philip and Ruth love her dearly. She has brought joy into our home and reminds us that the whole world is part of our family.

Dear brothers and sisters, we see daily about us unfathomable need. If only we had more powdered milk! If only we had more books! Yet we praise God for the good resources which He has entrusted to us.

May God's rich blessing continue with you in the New Year. Thank you for your prayers. Tell Sarah her good laugh carries all the way across the Pacific.

Love to all,
Daniel, Elnora, Philip and Ruth

Aunt Sarah sniffed into her handkerchief. Uncle Moses chuckled softly about Aunt Sarah's laugh. Cousin Paul looked thoughtful.

After several minutes of silence Grandfather spoke. "I believe the Christ Child Himself, Daniel's seven-year-old Ramsilla, has come to our Christmas feast. Do we have powdered milk and books for Him?"

"We think we're hard up this year, but the crops weren't a complete failure," Uncle 'Lijah added. "What about that sterilizer and refrigerator?"

Then Grandmother picked up the edges of her apron in gathering-eggs fashion and went around the room while the uncles dropped bills into it.

Hannah Elizabeth sat silent with wonder. Did Grandfather really think Ramsilla was the Christ Child come to their Christmas celebration? Wasn't that what he had said?

Late in the afternoon when the Shrocks were leaving, Hannah Elizabeth, bundled up for the trip home, found herself alone with Grandfather in the living room for a moment.

"Grandfather, I want to ask you something. This afternoon it seemed to me that the light from the Christmas star was shining into this very room. How do you know where a story ends and real life begins?"

Grandfather put his hand on her shoulder and looked at her in silence for a while. Then he said slowly, "We don't always know. You see things with an inner eye, little Hannah, and you have a way with words. Someday God will show you how to use these gifts."

Quick tears of joy misted Hannah Elizabeth's eyes, and she could not speak. Unwilling to cry in Grandfather's presence, she quickly stepped out onto the porch on the way to the car.

"Duck!" someone shouted. She plunged her head forward. Too late! Paul's well-aimed snowball spattered in the middle of her forehead.

❧ SIX

General Lee's Birthday

After the excitement of Christmas, January seemed like a vast Hoosier wasteland of ice and snow. Each day was a chunk of cold cut from this white expanse. No reunions. No Thanksgiving or Christmas feasts. No parties. Nothing at all until Valentine's Day.

Hannah Elizabeth pushed her nose and tongue against a frosty windowpane and pondered this intolerable situation. She was in the process of melting a circle in the frost feathers through which to look for the morning school bus. The children were to be at the roadside when the hack came, even in cold weather, so that the driver need not wait for them.

At her post as watchman Hannah Elizabeth observed the way the snow caught the sun in a million scintillating diamonds. She saw the icicles hanging from the eaves of the cozy house like stalactites in some fairy cave. Words began to tumble about and arrange themselves in her mind. She did not have to wait until she grew up to be a poet. She could begin now.

> Sunlight sparkles like diamonds
> On the *Ta-ta, Ta-ta* snow.
> Icicles hang like stalactites
> In a fairy cave aglow.

Where was the accent in "stalactites"? If it were on "lac," the whole line was sunk. And what kind of snow was it? Ta-ta, Ta-ta.

Hannah Elizabeth caught sight of the orange dot that would become the bus. "Hack's coming," she yelled. Timothy and Thomas grabbed caps and books and ran to the roadside. The three Shrocks were off into another school day.

Intermittently during the morning Hannah

Elizabeth worked on her poetry, answering questions in class discussion at the same time, or trying to. This was to be her downfall.

Fortunately for her line, the dictionary said *stalactite* could be accented on either the first or the second syllable. That was taken care of.

"Sunlight sparkles like diamonds on the *white and shining* snow." Hannah Elizabeth considered this possibility. Everyone knows, however, that snow is white; so why bother to say it? And, in a way, she had already said it was shining. Poets had to be careful about their words. Maybe she would say, "Sunlight sparkles

like diamonds on the *coldly glistening* snow."
She stared out the window. Somehow *coldly*
seemed too forbidding, like a proud queen,
and not pretty enough. "Sunlight sparkles like
diamonds on the *glistening, fairy* snow." No.
She could not use *fairy* twice.

The fifth-graders put away their reading
books and turned to arithmetic—all but one,
who sat staring, with her chin in cupped hands,
blithely unaware of this change. She was a pig-
tailed Diana, a mighty huntress of words. She
was skimming swiftly to far places in pursuit
of two elusive adjectives to describe what she
had seen. She did not hear a word that was
being said.

"Why is this done, Hannah Elizabeth?"

Hearing her name pronounced by Miss Davis
startled Hannah like a sudden clap of thunder.
The syllables Miss Davis had spoken were in
her ears, but she had to repeat them quickly to
herself to understand what they meant. "Why
is this done?" Hannah Elizabeth's braids jerked
as she gathered her wandering wits in an instant.

She knew exactly what was in that essay on "Conservation of Natural Resources."

"So that the furrows will keep the water from washing downhill," she answered clearly.

The fifth grade burst into laughter like a Fourth-of-July rocket exploding into sparks. Hannah Elizabeth's face felt hot as sunburn. What had she done? Oh, this was terrible!

Miss Davis rapped her pencil on her desk to bring the hilarious class to order.

"Hannah Elizabeth, we finished discussing that essay five minutes ago," Miss Davis said quietly. "It is all right to dream—at the right times and places. But you must not let dreaming keep you from knowing what is going on around you. I asked why we borrow ten instead of some other number in subtracting nineteen from thirty-one. Do you know?"

Hannah Elizabeth shook her head. She had not the faintest idea.

"What were you doing instead of listening to the explanation?" Miss Davis continued.

"I was trying to write something," Hannah Elizabeth said in a hard-to-talk voice.

Miss Davis walked down the aisle to Hannah Elizabeth's desk. She picked up the much-scribbled-on paper and read aloud:

Sunlight sparkles like diamonds
On the ... [She puzzled over the line]
   snow.
Icicles hang like stalactites
In a fairy cave aglow.

"Why, that's lovely," she said simply. "Someday you will be a poet. Your handwriting has improved too."

Hannah Elizabeth looked at Miss Davis and loved her boundlessly.

Living down the blunder was quite another matter. Why did she feel fiercely ashamed of having had her poem read aloud to everyone? It was like having a fragile, beautiful thing held up for people to laugh at. Maybe she would never be a poet at all just because of this incident. Because people had laughed at her. And it would be everyone else's fault.

Yet all the while she was thinking these dramatic thoughts, Hannah Elizabeth knew perfectly well that Miss Davis was right. She should have been listening to what was going on in class. If she failed to become a poet, it would be her fault, not anyone else's.

"Poet, poet, doesn't know it."

"You borrow ten so the furrow will keep the water from running down the hill!"

Hannah Elizabeth pretended to be angry at the teasing during recess, although she did not really mind. She immediately plunged with her classmates into a frenzy of planning, one of their favorite activities.

"We could have a two-day conference at our house on Friday and Saturday from nine to three," Hannah Elizabeth announced eagerly. Mennonites were always going to conferences to discuss religious matters.

"What would we do at this conference?" Roberta asked cautiously, for she had never heard of one.

"Well, we could do tricks and play games and give plays," Hannah Elizabeth continued enthusiastically. This would be a conference for fifth-graders.

"And eat," Patricia added. By now she too had caught the spirit.

"And eat," Hannah Elizabeth echoed Patricia, and her mind raced on. She thought of the Shrock family gatherings. "Each one who comes can bring food. In the afternoon we'll have a great dramatic production. I'll write a play about King Cophetua and the Beggar Maid."

"How can we have the conference on Friday when there's school that day?" Roberta asked. Hannah Elizabeth, not long on practicality, frowned. Roberta made the obvious decision. "We'll have it on Saturday only." Hannah Elizabeth was bossy. She had to be kept in check.

They decided to invite the boys and also to erect a dressing tent like the ones circus people have. They would sell ice-cream cones for a nickel apiece at a roadside stand in front of Hannah Elizabeth's house in order to make money. Would people buy ice-cream cones at a roadside stand in a snowy Indiana January? This question did not come up.

The conference provided planning material for several recesses, and the plans they made were as beautiful and fragile as the frost feathers on the windowpane through which Hannah Elizabeth had peered.

Whenever she had a free moment at school, Hannah Elizabeth worked diligently on a script for the conference play. She was careful this time. On her paper she wrote, "Never darken the king's door again." Aloud she said, "The main rivers of South America are the Amazon, the Orinoco and the Paraná–La Plata."

On Saturday at nine o'clock Hannah Elizabeth's mother was surprised to see Mrs. Thompson, a not-well-known neighbor, and her three children at the kitchen door. She handed Mrs. Shrock a large grocery bag of bananas and said, "The children especially mentioned that they were to bring food. This is so nice of you, Mrs. Shrock. I'm taking the chance to go to Kokomo to shop for the day. Good-by."

Before Mother Shrock quite realized that the three young Thompsons were now in her charge, their mother was on her way. Hannah Elizabeth suddenly felt a bit uncomfortable, especially as she saw the Hostetler girls arriving. Why hadn't it occurred to her to mention this conference to Mother? How many people had they invited? Thirty? Forty? Hannah Elizabeth's brow puckered, for numbers had a way of going hazy in her mind. What if everyone came? Mother had said something about finishing a dress today and washing heads, not to mention the usual Saturday work.

The Hostetler sisters knocked and handed Mother a package of store-bought cookies and a ring of bologna. They knew all about the system of bringing food. Whenever the Hostetlers went to a family gathering or to an all-day meeting at the church, they took along a basket full of food, just as the Shrocks did. Bruce Brown and two other Liberty boy playmates arrived empty-handed.

Hannah Elizabeth felt it prudent to avoid Mother Shrock. Anyway she had to get the Great Activities going in the living room. She did not succeed in the desired evasion. Mother confronted her when she was alone at the sewing machine taking a thimble from the drawer.

"Hannah Elizabeth Shrock . . ." There was a weighty pause. "Hannah Elizabeth Shrock, what does this mean?" The last four words were as crisp as well-fried bacon. "Is it someone's birthday or something?"

Fortunately—oh, joyful circumstance, oh, fortuitous deliverance—Hannah Elizabeth had looked at the calendar that very morning.

"Yes, it is, Mother. This is January 19. It's General Robert E. Lee's birthday."

General Lee? Did Mother perhaps feel weak? She only said, "Oh!" and set about dressing two chickens and making a freezer of ice cream. It occurred to Hannah Elizabeth that Mother was a very nice person. Did she enjoy "conferences" too? Her eyes looked sparkly, even if she acted resigned to an imperfect situation.

The Seth Thomas clock tumbled down from its shelf onto Joe Thompson's head while he was hunting for the thimble. During hide-and-seek Bruce Brown sat on the blackened upside-down iron pot in the hard-to-reach corner behind the cookstove. Mother used this old iron kettle for popping corn. She always removed a stove lid so that the round pot bottom was directly exposed to flame. And until this moment she had thought it quite out of the reach of children. But the crucially situated soot on Bruce Brown's trousers now proved otherwise —he, a well-cared-for only child.

The noon meal was a riot of joy. Such riddles! Such jokes! Such ice cream and cookies!

After the feast the conferees began rehearsing for *King Cophetua and the Beggar Maid.* Hannah Elizabeth agreed, with little urging, to be the beggar maid. Just who she had wanted to be when she wrote the script. But she had no idea of the good fortune that being the beggar maid would bring her.

Mother dispatched Timothy Joe to invite Mrs. Corry and the mothers of the boy playmates in Liberty to come to the performance.

"No admission charge. Refreshments served," her note said.

The tiny first-floor bedroom and slightly larger living room in the Shrock house were separated only by a curtained archway. Hannah Elizabeth's mother had made the two-piece cretonne pull drapery, perfect stage curtains. Her father had turned the wooden pull rod on his lathe. In fact, he had built the entire bedroom. A closet to the left of this archway and a dining-room entrance to the right made it a natural stage.

The idea of the play was, Hannah Elizabeth explained, that a mean courtier would try to drive the beggar maid away from the palace gate. He would say, "You good-for-nothing *shussle!*" Hannah Elizabeth and the Hostetler girls explained this Pennsylvania Dutch word to their playmates. They knew no single English word for "worthless, careless woman."

"You good-for-nothing *shussle!* Never darken the king's door again."

Just then the king—Bruce Brown in a bathrobe that covered his sooty seat—would come along, look at the beggar maid and say with a sigh, "I have never seen such beauty under the sun. This beggar maid shall be my queen! Bring her a royal gown!"

The rehearsal began.

"Food, please. Bread! Can you spare a penny for a poor beggar maid?" Hannah Elizabeth said imploringly, stretching out her arm.

"You good-for-nothing *shussle!*" Joe Thompson began vigorously, not pronouncing the vowel at all right.

Just then a pounding knock at the front door interrupted the practice.

"Who can it be?" Hannah Elizabeth wondered. All the Shrock friends came to the back door. They knew that the cracks around the front door were stuffed with rags to keep out the winter. "It must be a stranger."

Mother came from the kitchen, wiping her hands on her apron. She got the door open with difficulty, and the children became suddenly quiet as a bundled-up man with a black suitcase and merry eyes stepped into the crowded living room.

He looked around at the cast of strangely dressed children and then at Mother. Who was more surprised?

"Are all these children yours, ma'am?" he asked politely.

Hannah Elizabeth giggled in spite of herself. What was it about his words?

"No, they're not all mine," Mother answered, emphasizing the "all." Then, eyeing the black suitcase, she added, "I don't want to buy anything today."

"I come from a large family myself," he said cordially, ignoring her last remark and throwing his wraps over the back of a chair. " 'What you lack in money, you can always make up in children,' my old mother says." He nodded. "Yes, yes, children are the truest gold."

"That's right," Mother agreed. She had often thought of the idea, but had never heard it said in just those words.

"I'm Seumas O'Shea, and your name, ma'am?" the peddler inquired.

"Shamas O Shay!" Mother thought wonderingly. "Why doesn't he have a proper name like Jacob or John?" Aloud she said politely, "I'm Susan Shrock."

"Sure and I'm pleased to know you, Mrs. Shrock. Children are the truest gold," he repeated as he deftly opened the black bag.

The members of the "conference" stared at its contents. Green, red and brown bottles of all shapes and kinds. Mysterious boxes of many colors and sizes.

"I'm much obliged to you, but I don't need a thing," Mother tried to say firmly. There was only one dollar in the house.

Mr. Seumas O'Shea seemed not to have heard her, for he began to speak melodiously of the virtues of his wares. "I can tell by looking that you are a good cook, Mrs. Shrock." He unscrewed the cap from a bottle of vanilla and breathed deeply. "Ah, and did you ever smell such an aromatic fragrance?" Carefully waving

the bottle, he generously allowed all the members of the conference to get a tantalizing whiff.

"Ma'am, one teaspoonful of this vanilla equals four teaspoons of ordinary vanilla."

Hannah Elizabeth listened fascinated to the merry little waves in the stranger's words. Surely this was the best vanilla in the world! If Mother could only afford to buy a bottle!

"And these thimbles, needles and thread would help in the mending of this wee lady's dress," the peddler said reprovingly to Mother. He could not help noticing the rips and tears in the costume Hannah Elizabeth had found in the rag bag.

Hannah Elizabeth felt embarrassed for Mother's sake. Mother was one of the best seamstresses around. "Oh, Mr. Seumas O'Shea, we're giving a play. I'm the beggar maid. I'm wearing this torn dress on purpose," Hannah Elizabeth explained breathlessly. "Then I'll be the queen. I think your vanilla smells wonderful. It *does* have an ar-o-mat-ic fragrance."

The peddler laughed. "Sure and this wee

lady has a bit of blarney in her tongue. If she is a beggar maid, I must give her a present."

He selected something from his suitcase and handed it to Hannah Elizabeth, who in turn looked questioningly at Mother. Mother shrugged her shoulders and smiled.

"Oh, thank you, Mr. O'Shea," Hannah Elizabeth said fervently. One of her long, long wishes had come true. She was the proud owner of a tube of toothpaste.

"Now, Mrs. Shrock," Mr. Seumas O'Shea said sincerely, taking a flat brown box from his bag, "I want to show you something I don't show to ordinary customers. I can tell that you appreciate beauty. I can tell that these young actors and actresses appreciate beauty. This . . ." He carefully removed the box lid and held up by two corners a square piece of beige cloth.

"This is genuine Irish lace." He paused as the conference looked at the lace.

"Just look at the beauty of this pattern. In the corner of each square you see a wild Irish rose." He stroked the syllables with his voice as he said them. "In each corner you have a shamrock. Only an Irishman can appreciate the beauty of the shamrock." Mr. O'Shea gazed reverently into space. "And here you have the heart. They say a true Irish heart loves forever."

Hannah Elizabeth sighed as she looked at the lace. A true Irish heart loves forever! How poetic! Why did she have to have a plain old Pennsylvania Dutch heart?

"This lace is fit for a queen," the peddler continued, looking straight at Hannah Elizabeth and then at Mother.

"Now, Mrs. Shrock. I could not think of selling you this lace. Would I think of selling my own flesh and blood? This lace was made by the hands of my own old blind mother." Mr. O'Shea paused to blow his nose.

A sympathetic lump rose in Hannah Elizabeth's throat. Mother looked worried and sad. Bruce Brown looked embarrassed.

"I am her sole and only means of support," Mr. O'Shea added when he regained control of his nose. "I would not think of selling this lace.

But if you would give me only one dollar—I don't need to tell you it is worth much more—I would *give* you this lace. This genuine Irish lace made by the hands of my own dear mother."

Hannah Elizabeth looked pleadingly at Mother.

"Well, I believe I'll take it," Mother said simply. She went to the kitchen for the dollar and came back with a brown paper bag. "I do have a few eggs left, Mr. O'Shea. Would you please take them to your dear old mother?"

The peddler looked startled, but, being Mr. Seumas O'Shea, he rose to the occasion. He bowed gallantly to Mother. "Thank you kindly, ma'am. You have an Irish heart. A true Irish heart! On behalf of my mother, I thank you."

Then Mr. Seumas O'Shea left the Shrock house forever with his words and his wares. But Hannah Elizabeth never forgot him.

The "conference" played *King Cophetua and the Beggar Maid* to the neighbor women. Hannah Elizabeth wore the lace on her head in the last part of the play. The audience applauded appreciatively.

Mrs. Corry wiped the corners of her eyes with her handkerchief, explaining that both sad and happy stories made her cry. The women examined the lace and shook their heads when they found out how much Mother had paid for it. "Ay, ay, ay, Susan! A whole dollar! And it's not a bit prettier than your own crocheting. But why all the celebration today?" they wanted to know.

"Hannah Elizabeth says it's General Lee's birthday," Mother explained.

When Father came home from his long day's work, the house was not in its usual Saturday-night order. Hannah Elizabeth heard Mother tell him, "I didn't get the dress finished or a single pie baked. I'll tell you the story later. I think I cannot possibly get into the spirit for the Lord's Day."

In a dark room Hannah Elizabeth looked through a window at the early-winter night sky to do her daily philosophizing. Which was lovelier, those beautiful plans for today, or today itself? Patricia and Roberta had not even come to the conference. The circus tent and roadside stand had not materialized. But it had been a perfect day. Just perfect! They never could have planned Mr. Seumas O'Shea. The "Planning for a Thing to Happen" and the "Thing That Happened" were both wonderful. Just different, that was all.

How nice of General Lee to be born on January 19! Tomorrow would be Sunday. It was Grandfather's turn to preach. Perhaps he would tell the story of manna and quails in the wilderness or of water gushing from the rock. Perhaps he would read those verses from Psalm 46. January was an exciting month after all. She owned a tube of toothpaste. The lace was lovely. The stars were in the sky. God was in heaven. And Hannah Elizabeth was in the spirit for the Lord's Day.

⇘ SEVEN

"Whan That Aprille..."

Early in the spring Hannah Elizabeth's father tapped their six maple trees. Red-winged blackbirds sang in swampy tracts and along drainage ditches. Cardinal wings flashed by in the sun. To Hannah Elizabeth it seemed that joy flowed through the Hoosier countryside like tiny trickles of water through all the fields.

Hannah Elizabeth underlined in her Bible with a red pencil: *The mountains skipped like rams, and the little hills like lambs.* Perhaps people in church should quote this verse sometimes instead of using so often the one about being *a peculiar people zealous of good works.*

One afternoon when her part of the Saturday cleaning was done, Hannah Elizabeth slipped away to the woods, like a migrating bird sure of its springtime destination. Agilely she climbed a fence at the edge of the Shrock property. She crossed a new-plowed field of turned-over black furrows.

At night in her dreams Hannah Elizabeth floated over fields like these. It was a glorious feeling, light and easy as an apple-blossom petal.

Above her now a killdeer mounted and dipped swiftly. Hannah Elizabeth recalled the Ugly Duckling. *Oh, he could not forget those beautiful birds, those happy birds. He was quite beside himself. . . . He did not know what the birds were, or whither they flew, but all the same he was more drawn toward them than he had ever been by any creatures before.*

"Perhaps I can do it when I'm awake. Now! I've done it a hundred times," Hannah Elizabeth said for no one but herself and the killdeer to hear.

But, try as she would, Hannah Elizabeth could not fly. Her arms were powerless in air. Her feet remained in the good earth. She laughed aloud because she had tried to fly and because it was spring.

Hannah Elizabeth climbed another fence into a lane and dumped the soil from her shoes. She walked past two fields to reach the woods, uncleared heart of a section of Indiana farmland with Liberty at its corner. Later she would come again to the woods with members of her family to gather mushrooms, to picnic, to pretend with Timothy and Thomas that the pawpaw patch was a dense, impenetrable jungle. But now the woods would be hers alone. She breathed deeply and quickened her pace. What a relief not to have people around, making noises with their mouths, scaring birds away and not feeling how beautiful everything was.

So much to do in a woods in spring! Hannah Elizabeth used her nose. What did it smell like? Not like leaves rotting, although that seemed to be part of it. It smelled dank and alive, like things growing.

Hannah Elizabeth could never see enough in a spring woods. She loved the wild flowers, and she loved their names. In her old dictionary was a full page in color entitled "Wild Flowers of North America." From that page she had learned the words she spoke now: "hepatica, anemone, trillium."

She crossed the entrance clearing, rounded the pawpaw patch, got through the wild raspberry thicket with difficulty and stood motionless.

Spring beauties grew in profusion on this part of the woods floor. Hannah Elizabeth caught her breath, struck by a bolt of beauty. They were like a whole congregation of white and pale pink fairies singing a *Te Deum* of joy.

When Hannah Elizabeth got over the initial ecstasy, she slipped to her knees to examine one of the flowers closely. Pink lines ran through each of five pale pink petals to the tiny yellow stamens in the center. The leaves were tapering and slender, as befitted such fragile ladies.

"Oh, you are lovely, lovely!" Hannah Eliza-

beth whispered. "Hundreds of you." She wondered why God had placed so much beauty in
this woods where people seldom came. She sat
on a stump to think about it. Did God hide
things purposely? *There is a river, the streams
whereof make glad . . . make glad . . .* It all fitted
together somehow if she could only figure it
out. What was that river?

She moved on to observe other flowers. Only

a few of the wake-robins were open. In one section of the woods a whole host of green umbrellas, the mayapples, grew together. Mother said they were poison. Father said he used to eat their yellow berries when he was a boy. And he was still alive. Perhaps only the roots and leaves were poison. Were they or weren't they? Hannah Elizabeth wanted to know, but not badly enough to sample the leaves. It would be sad indeed to die here alone in the woods like those poor children the birds covered with strawberry leaves—the ones in a story which had made her sad when she was very young.

The thought startled Hannah Elizabeth. The sun was already resting on Mrs. Corry's Gingerbread House. Impossible! She would have to hurry to get home before dark.

When Hannah entered the warm-smelling kitchen at home, the table was already set. Mother was just taking cornbread out of the oven. Father was home from work and washing for supper at the washbasin in the corner of the kitchen.

"Our daughter spent the livelong afternoon in the woods by herself," Mother told him.

"A good day for it," he commented through his wet washcloth. "Maybe we can all go to hunt mushrooms tomorrow afternoon."

From her place at the table Hannah Elizabeth looked at her parents and loved them. They were not "fashionable" like her schoolmates' parents. But they were hers.

The cornbread tasted scrumptious to Hannah Elizabeth—steaming, yellow, mealy. She ate one piece with sugar and milk, the way Father ate his. She split open a second piece and spread butter, soon melted, on the two sides, the way Mother ate hers.

The family stayed at the table for worship. Father read:

God is our refuge and strength,
a very present help in trouble.
Therefore will not we fear,
though the earth be removed,
and though the mountains be carried
into the midst of the sea.

How comforting to know that God was sure and strong and good! His love was for all people, including the wide world beyond Liberty. All of them could feel happy and glad. Of this, Hannah Elizabeth felt sure.

❧ EIGHT

Easter Sunday

That year the Mennonite congregation held members' meeting on the Sunday afternoon before Easter. Brother Jacob, co-minister with Grandfather Shrock, preached the sermon on the usual text for this occasion: *"Let a man examine himself, and so let him eat of that bread and drink of that cup."*

He urged each member of the congregation to search his own life. Had any man anything against him? Then let him go to that man and make it right, lest any impurity sully the Lord's table on the Resurrection Day.

❧ *117*

Hannah Elizabeth watched Brother Jacob's beard move up and down as he talked. She scrutinized her own life. She had been jealous of Bruce Brown at school because he always got higher marks than she in arithmetic. Tomorrow she would say to him, "I'm glad you get good grades in arithmetic. I only wish I could do as well." She had skipped out on her share of dishwashing to read and to play the piano. She had stayed in the woods so long that Mother had had to set the table for her. She really would try to help more around the house from now on, and to be kinder to her brothers.

At the end of the sermon each member of the congregation went alone into the men's or women's anteroom at the back of the church and answered the questions asked by the ministers: "Are you, so far as you know, at peace with God and with the brotherhood? Are you ready to participate in the communion and feet-washing service next Sunday?"

Hannah Elizabeth wished fervently that she were old enough to be a member of the church, wear a white net covering like Mother's on her head during meetings, drink the grape juice and eat the bread of the communion service. About feet-washing she was not sure. It was another of those things that the "popular" churches in the towns did not do. Could she explain it to her schoolmates? Washing feet that were already clean and kissing the person afterward?

During the week the Shrock family dyed hard-cooked and raw eggs. Mother tapped tiny holes in both ends of the colored raw ones. She carefully blew out the whites and yolks, used them for cooking and saved the gaily colored shells for the annual egg tree.

On Easter Sunday morning the greening cherry tree, the one that had furnished a branch for the Christmas celebration, stood transformed on the front lawn. Its branches were tipped with yellow, pale blue, red, rose, lavender and aqua eggs. Hannah Elizabeth thought it the gayest tree in the world.

On the way to church Mother and Father were silent, anticipating the coming solemn celebration. Hannah Elizabeth looked admiringly at her new white shoes and wondered what Rachel's would be like.

Grandfather Shrock preached the Easter communion sermon. He spoke simply, movingly. "Beloved brothers and sisters, the separate grains of wheat were crushed to become flour. From the flour this bread is made to remind us of Christ's broken body. So in the body of Christ —that is, the church—we are all one. We are not separate grains of wheat, but members of one another.

"The separate grapes are crushed to become this juice, which reminds us of the shed blood of Christ. Let us eat this bread and drink this wine with solemn joy in remembrance of our crucified and risen Lord."

Sunlight streamed through the plain glass windows. Hannah Elizabeth, sitting with other girls on a familiar wooden bench toward the front of the church, chanted inwardly, *"There is a river, the streams whereof shall make glad . . . make glad . . ."*

How she loved Grandfather and his beautiful

words! How she loved Grandmother, sitting quietly with the older women in the "Amen corner." How could anyone be so quiet?

Now Grandfather, Brother Jacob and their helpers moved noiselessly among the waiting members of the congregation, handing them bits of broken bread. From time to time Grandfather said softly and reverently, *"This do in remembrance of me."* After cups of sweet wine had been distributed, Grandfather returned to the pulpit to speak of the feet-washing ceremony which would follow.

"Why did Peter say to the Master, '*Not my feet only, but also my hands and my head!'?* Peter did not understand what Jesus was doing. He did not understand that this was a sublime object lesson that would go down through the centuries to the end of time. In sweet humility we are to serve one another, beloved. *'If ye know these things, happy are ye if ye do them.'* "

Soon the sound of gently splashing water sounded through the church. Members of the congregation had paired off and were washing one another's feet at small tin tubs placed along

the outside aisles, men on one side, women on
the other.

Hannah Elizabeth looked at the feet of the
women at the tub nearest her. Those feet looked
as though they had been in black shoe prisons

a long time. Hannah Elizabeth wanted to giggle at the shape of some of those feet. What if you were ticklish? she wondered. But she quickly stifled such thoughts, for the grownups were deeply serious.

Feet-washing sounded all right the way Grandfather explained it. "In sweet humility we are to serve one another, beloved." Probably that was what Mother was doing when she washed for people who were ill or took a jar of soup to Mrs. Corry. Probably that's what the uncles were doing when they made hay or plowed a field for a neighbor who was ill.

As the gentle splashing continued, a voice began to sing. Others joined in. Soon the church reverberated with song.

Extol the love which sought to show
The Father's boundless grace;
The Son, from Father's bosom came,
Beheld the Father's face;—
In servile garments clothed upon,
With humble service meet,
The Master loved as none could love
And washed His servants' feet.

123

When this song ended, another was begun. The singing continued until all members had washed feet with another. The meeting closed with the singing of joyous Easter hymns. "He is risen! He is risen!"

Immediately after the benediction, the heightened solemn feeling so in evidence during the meeting seemed to break. A relaxed buzz of friendly visiting took its place. The children, Hannah Elizabeth especially, tensed with excitement anticipating the family gatherings that would follow.

"I have an important secret to tell you at Grandpa's," Rachel, her eyes sparkling, whispered to Hannah Elizabeth.

The heavily laden table at Grandfather's house looked as it had on Christmas Day, except for the abundance of eggs. Bowls of gaily decorated eggs in the shell adorned the table. Grandmother, Mother and various aunts had during the week filled crocks with beets, vinegar and shelled hard-cooked eggs. Glass dishes of these tart beets and red eggs added festive color to the Easter feast.

Hannah Elizabeth and Rachel again took their plates to the upstairs room that had given them privacy on Christmas Day. "What is it, Rachel? What is it?" Hannah Elizabeth begged her cousin.

"I'm trying to tell you," Rachel said, "if you'll only let me talk. We're going to have a baby next summer. If it's a boy, Paul gets to name him. If it's a girl, I get to name her!" Rachel finished triumphantly.

At that moment Hannah Elizabeth turned into a blob of jealousy. A baby! Aaron would not let her hold him at all anymore. He was a boy, not a baby.

"Could I help name her, please, please, please, Rachel?" Hannah Elizabeth begged.

"I don't know," Rachel said smugly. "You might call her Christine Evangeline Penelope Antoinette, and that's too much name for a baby." This is what Hannah Elizabeth called her favorite paper doll.

"It's a beautiful name," Hannah Elizabeth countered, tossing her pigtails. "Besides, it will probably be a boy."

During the afternoon Grandfather moved with obvious happiness among his many sons and daughters and their children. He was not yet old, but already he was beginning to reap a golden harvest in his family, in his congregation and community. He had never traveled far from this farm. But he knew that you do not go away to find happiness. You find it where you are or not at all. God wanted him here. That was enough. *"The lines are fallen unto me in pleasant places; yea, I have a goodly heritage,"* he said.

Grandfather was teaching a group of older boy cousins to play finger tricks with string when Rachel and Hannah joined them.

"We have enough here for everyone." He smiled, giving each of the girls a hank of string.

Hannah Elizabeth learned to "pull the string through" by putting it around her neck, holding the looped ends in her two forefingers, quickly slipping one finger out of its loop into the other and pulling the string out straight. The making of crows' feet escaped her altogether, however.

Her string became a hopeless tangle, and she got bothered inside trying to straighten it out.

"It's easy!" boasted Cousin Paul, exhibiting two perfect, joined webs of string. "You girls!" he added scornfully.

"We do different things well." Grandfather smiled. "Paul here has much skill in his hands and may someday be a missionary doctor like his Uncle Daniel. Hannah Elizabeth will be my poet."

Hannah Elizabeth stopped struggling with her string. What if she couldn't make crows' feet? What if she didn't get to name a baby? It was like the Ugly Duckling. What if she couldn't *lay eggs, arch her back, purr, or give off sparks!* Grandfather loved her anyway. And he believed that she would become a poet!

❧ NINE

Here No Continuing City

The next morning Hannah Elizabeth was awakened by an unfamiliar voice in the kitchen below her bedroom. This was unheard of! What could Uncle 'Lijah be doing here early on Monday morning? She tiptoed softly down the stairs to eavesdrop.

Uncle 'Lijah spoke in Pennsylvania Dutch. "Father died this morning."

Mother's coffeepot stopped in mid-air.

"It can't be true!" Father exclaimed. "He's never been sick a day in his life. Yesterday . . ."

"He slumped forward at the table as he was

eating breakfast a while ago," Uncle 'Lijah said
quietly. "Heart attack. Mother wants the sons
and daughters to come home this morning to
make plans."

"What about the children?" Mother wanted
to know.

"They should go to school today and tomorrow as usual," Uncle 'Lijah said. "Father would
want it that way."

When Hannah Elizabeth stepped into the
kitchen, Father and Mother were ready to go
with Uncle 'Lijah. "Grandfather Shrock went
home to heaven this morning," Father said
simply.

"We are going to Grandmother," Mother
added. "See to it that the boys are ready for
school. We'll take Aaron with us."

Hannah Elizabeth ate her breakfast oatmeal in
silence. She suddenly felt close to a great adventure. Death. What had it to do with her and
with Grandfather?

That day, absorbed in her school world, Hannah Elizabeth scarcely thought of Uncle 'Lijah's

morning message. At recess she, Patricia, Roberta and half a dozen other girls skipped rope until the bell rang. They skipped through school. They took turns doing:

> Teddy bear, teddy bear, turn around.
> Teddy bear, teddy bear, touch the ground.

In the middle of the gay chant Hannah Elizabeth wondered, "Is it right to be so happy today when Grandfather Shrock is dead?"

That evening Hannah Elizabeth's family drove once more down the lane to Grandfather's house. The lane itself was lined with cars and an occasional Amish buggy.

Inside the house, church people, neighbors and relatives either sat in silence or talked about Joseph Shrock. How sudden his passing was! With what unforgettable power he had preached yesterday! How fitting that his children and their families—all except Daniel—had been with him the day before! Who could take his place in the pulpit and in their hearts? How lonely it would be for Sister Hannah. Would she soon move into the little house? Which of the children would move into the big house and take over the farm?

Hannah Elizabeth went into the bedroom and looked at the familiar form lying there in the casket. Only yesterday this body had moved among them. This lifeless body was not Grandfather. Hannah Elizabeth felt sure of that. Where was he? She dried her eyes with her handkerchief.

On the Wednesday afternoon of the funeral the plain white country meetinghouse was crowded. The family had requested that friends who wished to do so send monetary gifts to the hospital in India as a memorial to Grandfather rather than spend money for flowers. Many did both. Hannah Elizabeth, Rachel and the other granddaughters, older and younger than they, carried bouquets down the aisle.

Six strong grandsons, Paul among them, carried the casket into the church. On it was a single sheaf of wheat. Uncle Moses, the oldest son, walked with Grandmother. Behind them came the other sons and daughters and their families, arranged according to age.

The congregation sang a hymn. Sunlight streamed through the plain glass windows. Everything seemed familiar and comfortable to Hannah Elizabeth. God was the same today as he had been yesterday. Sunday, communion and feet-washing; today, a funeral, Grandfather's funeral. Death was a part of life.

Rachel turned her head and slipped a smile to Hannah Elizabeth. Hannah wanted to return it but was not sure it would be proper to smile at Grandfather's funeral. Instead she looked soberly at the tips of her Easter shoes.

Brother Jacob rose to say, "At the request of our bereaved sister I shall read the Psalm our brother read aloud at the table shortly before his home-going. Psalm 46.

> God is our refuge and strength,
>   a very present help in trouble.
> Therefore will not we fear,
>   though the earth be removed,
>   and though the mountains be carried
>   into the midst of the sea;

Though the waters thereof roar and be troubled,
 though the mountains shake
  with the swelling thereof. Selah.
There is a river,
  the streams whereof shall make glad
   the city of God,
  the holy place of the tabernacles
   of the most High. . . .

Hannah Elizabeth slid to the edge of the wooden church bench. She felt exultant and dismayed at the same time. Why hadn't she realized all along that Grandfather knew what the river was? He had been reading about it just before he died. Why hadn't she asked him what it was? Oh, why hadn't she asked him? It was too late now.

Brother Jacob read the obituary. A visiting minister preached the funeral sermon on the text: *Here have we no continuing city, but we seek one to come.*

Those were the very words Grandfather had said to Hannah Elizabeth last autumn, the day she could not milk Dolly and got supper instead. Grandfather had known all along that he would die, that he would not stay on this earth forever. Now he had gone down a lane somehow into another world to a city God had built. A city made glad by a stream.

Hannah Elizabeth kept thinking about that 46th Psalm. *God is our refuge and strength. . . .* The first part of it was clearly about God. About how strong and helpful he was, no matter what terrible things were happening. *There is a river, the streams whereof shall make glad . . . .* The next part of the Psalm must also be about God. Hannah Elizabeth wriggled excitedly. Suddenly she felt alone on a stump in the woods with spring beauties nodding all around her.

That was it! The river and its streams must be God flowing along with you every day. Then everything is glad all the time, even if it is difficult or sorrowful. *The river was the presence of God.* It was not a real river with water in it. She had figured it out.

The river and its streams could be anywhere, everywhere. It could be at school, in Mrs. Dargent's apartment, at home, in a spring woods or here at Grandfather Shrock's funeral in the meetinghouse. This river was at both ends of Grandfather's lane. It was in life; it was in death. The river was for everyone. The fourth-grade teacher and Miss Davis. The Dargents and the Browns. Mrs. Corry. Seumas O'Shea. It was for her own family and church people. It was for Ramsilla and the people Uncle Daniel knew on the other side of the world.

Hannah Elizabeth could have shouted for joy at this new knowledge. "You don't shout for joy at funerals. You cry," she reprimanded herself.

When the chorister announced the hymn, Hannah Elizabeth realized that her mind had been wandering again. Other than the beginning text, she had heard not a word of the funeral sermon. At Grandmother's request the congregation sang Grandfather's favorite hymn, "Joyful, Joyful, We Adore Thee." Hundreds of people, among them Miss Davis, the Dargents and Mrs. Corry, filed by the open casket to view

Grandfather's body for the last time. Then the funeral was over.

A line of cars drove to the country cemetery, surrounded by newly sown fields. Hannah Elizabeth saw the casket placed above the grave. She heard the visiting minister read, *"If in this life only we have hope in Christ, we are of all men most miserable. But now is Christ risen from the dead and become the firstfruit of them that sleep."*

Eleven of Grandfather's twelve children and their families gathered at the farm homestead that evening to eat the meal the women of the congregation had prepared. Rachel and Hannah Elizabeth took their plates to the front-porch swing. To them this seemed like Christmas, Easter or any other family holiday.

At school the next day Miss Davis said to Hannah Elizabeth, "Your grandfather's funeral was like a worship service. What lovely faces the older women in your church have."

Lovely faces? What was Miss Davis talking about? They had the most ordinary faces in the world.

Before Hannah Elizabeth took her next piano lesson, Mrs. Dargent said to her, "It's hard to believe that people in your church sing all four parts so beautifully without a piano or organ. The Beethoven number was wonderful."

Hannah Elizabeth had never noticed who wrote the music to "Joyful, Joyful." What was Mrs. Dargent talking about?

When she took a half-dozen eggs to Mrs. Corry, Mrs. Corry said, "Who would have thought that your grandfather would go before I did!" This remark Hannah Elizabeth understood.

TEN

Hannah Delight

The next time Uncle 'Lijah came calling on a Monday morning, it was for quite a different reason. His face shone. "We have two girls now," he told Mother at the washing machine.

"Congratulations!" Mother said, drying her soapy hands on her apron so that she could shake his hand heartily. Her face too was radiant.

"Seven pounds and three ounces. Born last night at eleven o'clock. Everything is all right," Uncle 'Lijah continued.

"What's her name? What's her name?

What's her name?" Hannah Elizabeth wanted to know.

"I expect you'll like it all right," Uncle 'Lijah told his bouncing niece. "Rachel named her Hannah Delight."

Hannah Delight! How perfect! It sounded like all the stars dancing in the sky. Hannah Elizabeth was herself doing a kind of dance.

Uncle 'Lijah laughed. "Susan, I came to see whether you would let Hannah Elizabeth come along home with me to help Rachel cook for us menfolks until Ellen and the baby get home on Thursday," Uncle 'Lijah said to Mother.

"Oh, Mother, please. May I? May I?"

Mother looked amused. "If you really want her to, I suppose she can come."

The words were scarcely spoken when Hannah Elizabeth began tossing clothes into the battered family suitcase.

With so much new responsibility, Rachel and Hannah Elizabeth swelled like bantam hens puffing out their feathers. They were in charge of the household.

"Father says we can cook anything we can find in the garden or on the cupboard and cellar shelves," Rachel told her cousin. "What shall we have for dinner?"

"Let's look around the garden," Hannah Elizabeth suggested. Out of so many possibilities, how did one ever decide what to cook for a particular meal?

"Plenty of beets and spinach here," Rachel observed.

"Let's have spinach for dinner and beets for supper."

"All right. Do you know how to cook spinach?"

"Well, I suppose so. I think you cover it with water, salt it and cook it just like you do potatoes."

"We can't have just spinach for dinner," Rachel said.

The girls searched the cupboard shelves and found a package of rice.

"How many of us are there?" Hannah Elizabeth wanted to know. "That doesn't look to me like much rice."

"Father and Paul, two of us and the little boys. That's six," Rachel counted. "If we cook all of it, it may be enough. I think it swells." The statement was prophetic.

The girls brought up from the cellar a quart of peaches for dessert and two quarts of beef which Aunt Ellen had canned at butchering time. They had only to place the beef into a skillet and heat it. But this turned out to be more difficult than they had anticipated. Both rubber jar rings tore, making the zinc lids hard to remove. And they had to dig the beef out of the jars with a paring knife.

They put the rice and spinach into two separate saucepans, salted them, covered both with water and put them on the stove to cook.

After a while Hannah Elizabeth said to Rachel, "Something has happened to the water on the rice. It's just disappeared. What shall we do?"

"We'll have to put more water on it."

"It's boiling over. What shall we do?"

"Looks like too much for that pan. Let's put some of it into another pan."

"It's scorched on the bottom. What shall we do?"

"Let's throw the scorched part away."

"We need another pan."

"I didn't know rice was so hard to cook, did you?"

Meanwhile the spinach bubbled away. "It looks kind of funny," Hannah Elizabeth said, lifting the lid.

"It will be okay," Rachel said firmly, trying to bolster their sagging confidence.

Uncle 'Lijah asked the blessing at the dinner table. As soon as the "amen" was finished and the food passed, the little boys began to eat with gusto. They had stomachs like billy goats. Now as always they ate what was served to them and spoke only to ask for more. But Cousin Paul had reached a more discriminating age. He started commenting on the food.

"Gee whiz! What's that green water?"

"That's spinach," Rachel said with dignity.

"Spinach! It doesn't look like spinach to me. Gee whiz!"

"Watch your language, Paul," Uncle 'Lijah admonished.

Hannah Elizabeth was incensed. "We eat it at our house all the time," she told him.

"I feel sorry for your family. It looks like green dishwater to me. Why did you cook so much rice? Do you think you're cooking for thrashers?"

"I've never tasted better beef," Uncle 'Lijah said enthusiastically, trying to guide the conversation into constructive channels. "What shall I tell Mother for you when I see her this afternoon?"

Paul ignored his father's question. "Anyone can open cans."

The girls' eyes flashed volcanic fire.

"This is a complicated menu," Uncle 'Lijah said. "The girls have done well"—his eyes twinkled—"considering everything. For tonight let's have just one thing. You can put this leftover meat into a kettle, add vegetables—potatoes, carrots, onions—and have stew."

This sounded fine to the girls.

At the close of the meal Paul waited until
Uncle 'Lijah was out of earshot to make a final
remark. "Look at all these dirty dishes. Did
you use every pan in the house? I'm glad I don't
have to wash them."

"You'd just better watch out, Paul Shrock,"
Rachel said with menace in her tone.

The girls washed the dishes and spent the rest of the afternoon practicing a piano duet and swinging on a long hay rope in the barn. This rope was used with a pulley at haying time to swing bales of hay into place in the haymow. The girls took turns holding the rope, jumping from the mow and swinging back and forth across the open middle space of the barn until the "old cat died."

Too soon, it seemed, it was time to prepare the evening meal. Hannah Elizabeth and Rachel followed Uncle 'Lijah's directions for making stew with one exception. Since they had earlier planned to have beets for supper, they decided to add a few to the stew. They peeled the beets as they did the potatoes, staining their hands in the process. The only drawback to the addition of the beets was that everything in the kettle—carrots, potatoes, onions—turned a rather startling shade of red.

"It tastes all right," Hannah Elizabeth said cautiously, sampling their product, "even though it does look a little queer."

At supper Paul began, "Gee whiz!"

"Paul," Uncle 'Lijah said. "Didn't Mother tell you to eat whatever the girls set before you?"

"I don't think she knew they'd set this kind of stuff before me," Paul said glumly. "Did they dump a bottle of red food coloring into it?"

"Do you think it's right to thank God for the food at the beginning of the meal and spend the rest of the time grumbling about it?" Uncle 'Lijah asked. "Close your eyes and eat it. It *tastes* delicious."

"Tastes all right even when your eyes are open," one of the little brothers said with his mouth full of stew.

"Now, I don't want to hear another word of complaining, Paul," Uncle 'Lijah admonished. "Today, tomorrow, or the next day. Not one word. Do you understand?"

Paul understood.

Hannah Elizabeth and Rachel plotted over their dishpans. They had had quite enough of Paul.

Next morning the two cooks sat piously at the breakfast table, not hearing one word of the chapter Uncle 'Lijah read from the Bible for morning devotions.

How beautiful that breakfast looked! Marshmallows bobbing in cups of cocoa, slices of buttered toast on a large platter and at each place an almost perfectly fried egg.

At the end of the "amen" Paul gulped some cocoa and set his cup down, sputtering. "Gee whiz!" he said.

Uncle 'Lijah looked at him ominously. "Paul!"

Paul was silent, for Uncle 'Lijah was not easily disobeyed.

Rachel and Hannah Elizabeth ate with a sweetness more natural to Grandmother than to them.

Uncle 'Lijah drank his cocoa with relish. Paul looked at him and was filled with involuntary admiration for his father. How could any mortal be so magnanimous!

Paul forked a bite of egg to his mouth. Ugh!

With lowered eyelids the girls watched his facial contortions and kicked each other under the table. Hannah Elizabeth turned her head to cough into her hand. The little boys were eating too heartily to notice that anything was amiss.

"Would you please pass the salt, Rachel?" Uncle 'Lijah asked his daughter.

As Paul watched Uncle 'Lijah sprinkle salt on his egg, a great light dawned. He glared at the girls across the table.

"Dad," he said, selecting his words with care, "it . . . does not seem . . . fair. . . ."

Uncle 'Lijah ignored this remark. "After breakfast Rachel and Hannah Elizabeth may ride along when I take the little boys to Aunt Paton Ruth's." This aunt was called by her husband's name to distinguish her from two other Ruth aunts. "You boys will spend the day there. Paul, you are to stay here and do the breakfast dishes."

"Gee—"

"You can go along to town this afternoon," Uncle 'Lijah added, trying to soften the blow.

"We'll see about getting flash attachments for your camera."

"Flash attachments! I don't have enough money saved yet!" Uncle 'Lijah's remark suspended Paul between a north pole and a south pole of feeling, a loathing for dirty dishes and his heart's dearest desire.

By this time the yeast in Hannah Elizabeth's conscience was beginning to rise. Should they have dumped all that salt into Paul's cocoa and egg?

When Uncle 'Lijah commended the girls' work to Aunt Paton Ruth later in the morning, Hannah Elizabeth felt ashamed.

Aunt Paton Ruth sent home with Uncle 'Lijah a dish of baked beans, a gelatin salad and a raspberry pie. "For your dinner," she told him. She gave Rachel and Hannah Elizabeth each a dime "for being such good workers."

Paul ate with gusto at noon. "Tastes good to have decent food again," he said.

Poor Paul! Hannah Elizabeth felt smitten. All that salt for breakfast. How could she make up for playing such a mean trick?

"Paul," Hannah Elizabeth said, when she could speak to him alone as he was heading toward the stairway to dress for the trip to town. "Here's a dime to help you buy your flash attachment."

Paul looked longingly at the dime. A flash attachment cost a lot of money. Every little bit helped. He straightened his shoulders. After all, he did not take money from little girls, even if they did . . .

"No, thank you," he said with a tender gruffness. "I don't really need it."

Hannah Elizabeth looked disappointed.

Paul had an inspiration. "Tell you what, though. I could use a nickel. I'll bring you the change."

On Thursday morning Hannah Elizabeth and Rachel cleaned the house until it shone. They scrubbed and rubbed. They dusted and swept. They fluffed pillows and changed sheets. This was to be Hannah Delight's homecoming day. Hannah Elizabeth and Rachel took baths, put on clean clothes and braided each other's hair in eager anticipation. What would she be like? Hannah Delight! Hannah Delight!

Aunt Ellen seemed overjoyed to be home again. She exclaimed about how clean the house looked. She listened and laughed at the little boys' stories of their good time at Uncle Paton's. She told Paul how proud she was of the way he had done the chores.

After Rachel had had her turn, Aunt Ellen asked Hannah Elizabeth, "Would you like to rock your little namesake?"

"Oh, could I really!" Stars danced in Hannah Elizabeth's eyes. Just what she had been longing to do! But she had not dared ask for so great a privilege.

"Hannah Delight! Hannah Delight!" the rocking-chair rungs seemed to sing as she rocked her newest cousin. How could she have thought all babies looked alike? She would know this baby in a hundred babies. What soft black hair! Rings of it! What a tiny nose! And those curling little hands! Now the baby was yawning and gazing around. She trusted Hannah Elizabeth completely Oh, bliss! Oh, joy!

"She won't vanish into thin air," Aunt Ellen laughed. "We'll put her into her basket now so that she can sleep."

That night Hannah Elizabeth's parents came for her, bringing along Grandmother Shrock and her suitcase.

"We'd like to trade one Hannah for another," Father announced.

"And we'd especially like to see the littlest Hannah," Mother added.

"I'm going to take a picture of all three Hannahs with the new flash attachment Father helped me buy," Paul said proudly. And he did.

Uncle 'Lijah introduced Hannah Delight to a few of her numerous relatives with obvious pride. He, a tenth-generation American, put his tiny daughter on his knee and in the time-honored nursery-horse fashion chanted to her in the language of the European Palatinate:

> *Ridey, ridey, guiley,*
> *Hahlf un stunt un miley.*
> *Mia vill mir havva dresha.*
> *No kan guiley havva fressa.*
> *Blump! Fahlas see nunna.*

> (Ride, little horsie,
> Half a mile an hour.
> Tomorrow we will thresh the hay.
> Then our colt can eat all day.
> Blump! She falls down.)

"Isn't she a little young for that, 'Lijah?" Aunt Ellen laughed.

"How will we know which Hannah Shrock we mean?" Mother asked.

"We'll call them Joe's Hannah, Mark's Hannah and 'Lijah's Hannah," Uncle 'Lijah said. "That is, until Hannah Elizabeth and Hannah Delight are married and become someone else's Hannahs."

"That won't be long." Grandmother smiled with dreams in her eyes.

Hannah Elizabeth puckered her forehead. Grownups again! Couldn't they see that it would be ages until Hannah Delight would be old enough to start to school, to say nothing of getting married. As for herself, she would never marry at all. How could you be a poet if you were married?

"We'd like to invite you folks to have supper with us two weeks from tomorrow night to celebrate Hannah Elizabeth's eleventh birthday," Mother said as they prepared to leave. "You come too, Mother Shrock."

"We'll bring the birthday cake and a freezer of ice cream," said Aunt Ellen.

"You don't need to," Mother assured her. But she knew they would.

⚹ ELEVEN

Eleven Candles

On Hannah Elizabeth's eleventh birthday she went alone to the woods, to the stump where she had pondered about spring beauties and *the river* in April. She wanted to think about being eleven, about growing older, about the past year. She wanted to anticipate her evening birthday celebration and the coming Shrock Reunion.

Grandfather was gone now, but his words were still in her heart. It had not been hard to explain feet-washing to Roberta and Patricia at school when she used Grandfather's words: *"in* loving humility we are to serve one another." Where was Grandfather now? He was in *a city whose builder and maker is God.* Was that city out somewhere among all the stars and planets? It did not matter where it was so long as the river was there making the city glad.

Hannah Elizabeth watched two tiny azure butterflies flutter by her stump. Now she knew about *the river, the streams whereof shall make glad the city of God,* but she had no one at all to talk to about it. Perhaps someday there would be people to tell.

If only she could know everything she wanted to know and do everything she wanted to do now that she was eleven. A blue jay screeched. She still couldn't hit a ball with a bat. She couldn't make crows' feet out of string. She couldn't milk a cow. She made mistakes in arithmetic, but her handwriting had improved. She was not beautiful, although she no longer minded her freckles because wonderful Miss Davis had them too. She spilled and knocked things over. Oh, dear!

Hannah Elizabeth squashed a mosquito on her bare leg. "It doesn't matter at all!" she told herself resolutely. "I can memorize poetry. I'll say a poem at Shrock Reunion. Miss Davis said I will be a poet. Grandfather said so too. I'll start writing a book of poems today on my eleventh birthday."

Maybe she was a swan. Maybe she was! Maybe God needed Ugly Ducklings who would someday turn into swans. Otherwise why did He make them? Maybe someday the children would say, "There is a new one! Yes, a new one has come. The new one is the prettiest of all!"

A rabbit bounced across the woods floor. The mosquitoes had found a tasty morsel. Hannah Elizabeth gave up battling them and returned home.

The birthday supper was a huge success—almost. Hannah Delight had hiccups. The guest of honor upset a glass of water onto the tablecloth. Uncle 'Lijah only laughed and said, "We wouldn't want things to be too dry and dull at a birthday party."

Paul took a flash picture of Hannah Elizabeth and her cake with its eleven lighted candles. Paul was all right. He had not called her Hanny Lizard for a long time.

Uncle 'Lijah's family gave her a brand-new dictionary. "Your mother said you wanted one," Aunt Ellen explained. It's partly to pay you for being such good help when I was in the hospital with Hannah Delight."

Bruce Brown sent her a birthday card. Mrs. Corry gave her a silver dollar. Grandmother Shrock gave her a hand-crocheted pot holder. Mother and Father gave her a blue plaid dress that Mother had made. The smallest package held a tube of toothpaste. "From Timothy, Thomas and Aaron," the label said.

What perfect presents! Just perfect! Hannah Elizabeth could hardly wait to begin reading the dictionary, although she did not mention this aloud. She would wear the dress to Shrock Reunion. The toothpaste Seumas O'Shea had given the beggar maid was almost gone. And what couldn't you buy with a silver dollar— if you chose to spend it?

At Shrock Reunion two weeks later Great-Uncle M.S. Shrock emerged from wherever he spent the rest of the year to be master of ceremonies. He made rambling remarks about "a heritage to pass on." He read a list of people who had died, beginning with "our beloved cousin Joseph Shrock." He read a list of people who had married. He asked who was the youngest person in the audience.

Aunt Ellen said, "Our Hannah Delight will be five weeks old tomorrow."

"Hannah Delight Shrock, five weeks old tomorrow," Great-Uncle M.S. announced in sonorous tones.

Were those peacocks sitting on either side of Aunt Ellen? No. They were just girls, two girls who were absolutely certain that not another baby in the whole world was half as pretty as theirs.

After much reminiscing and moralizing, Great-Uncle M.S. turned the meeting over to Cousin Eva. She looked into her black notebook and announced that Rachel Shrock would play a piano solo called "Airplanes in Flight." The piano was still out of tune. It bothered Hannah Elizabeth. The audience and Rachel did not seem to mind. The audience clapped. Rachel curtsied. She was beautiful. Just beautiful.

Cousin Eva announced that Hannah Elizabeth

Shrock would "speak a piece." Hannah Elizabeth said in clear tones, not mouthing words as some do, *"It is not growing like a tree in bulk doth make man better be. . . ."* The audience clapped. She curtsied. Even though that rusty nail still protruded from the third wooden step to the platform, Hannah Elizabeth returned to her seat without incident.

The next day after church Rachel and Hannah Elizabeth went home with Grandmother Shrock. Under her direction they learned to make potato salad, putting just the right amount of vinegar and sugar into the sour-cream dressing.

After dinner the girls popped corn and played in the attic. They played the piano. They practiced the alto part to "Joyful, Joyful, We Adore Thee."

At church that night Uncle Paton read Hannah Elizabeth's Psalm. *"God is our refuge and strength. . . . There is a river, the streams whereof shall make glad the city of God. . . ."* Hannah Elizabeth smiled.

Format by Robin Sherwood
Set in Linotype Janson
Composed by Wolf Composition Company, Inc.
Printed by Rae Publishing Company
Bound by Haddon Bindery, Inc.
HARPER & ROW, PUBLISHERS, INCORPORATED

O

Date D